... there is, for example, that it is a scene where she is
... involves long shot. The director was prepared to
... in big trouble because the temperature of the water
... short shot. Certainly, the shots would not be as
... camera and had to stay far enough away for ...
... of a scene. The distinction drawn, the scene befell. ...

SINCERELY, RONALD REAGAN

by

Helene von Damm

GREEN HILL PUBLISHERS, INC.
Ottawa, Illinois 61350

SINCERELY, RONALD REAGAN

Copyright © 1976 by Helene von Damm

ISBN: 0-916054-05-5

Library of Congress Catalogue Card Number 76-3355

Printed in the United States of America

First Printing, February 1976—150,000 copies
Second Printing, May 1976—30,000 copies
Third Printing, November 1976—26,000 copies
Fourth Printing, February 1977—25,000 copies
Fifth Printing, October 1977—27,000 copies

Green Hill Publishers, Inc.
Post Office Box 738
Ottawa, Illinois 61350

Contents

Foreword

Reading these letters restored my faith in the good sense of our people despite the deliberate confusion sown by the ax grinders. Our workaday citizens know honesty when they see it and hear it. It comes over loudly and clearly, when my old friend Ronnie rears up and delivers, as only he can, the facts and figures so necessary to the understanding of our economic and political situation.

No other politician that I've heard has performed that all important service with such clarity and courage.

The letters to the Governor prove the concurrence of the writers. Their numbers will grow in 1976.

Whatever course he chooses I know will be the sensible one and the best one for our Country. I am proud to call him my friend.

—James Cagney, August 1975

Introduction

I little thought when I arrived in America from Austria that less than ten years later I would be working for the governor of our nation's most populous state, taking his dictation, transcribing his letters, setting his daily schedule, and doing the hundred other things a personal secretary must do to make her boss's day as easy and as effective as possible.

And I never dreamed that one day I would even be speaking on his behalf or, finally, putting together a book of his correspondence; letters not only to prominent people but also to those fine men, women, and children whom nobody has ever heard of but who really make our country what it is.

I am grateful to the governor for letting me go through and select the letters from him, and in some cases to him, that I think reveal better than anything else possibly could the real Ronald Reagan—the man, his beliefs, his principles, and his character.

Since this is a book of letters, I thought perhaps a letter I wrote in 1974 in response to a question about my position might tell the story. The letter was written to Mrs. Harriet Johnson, chairman of the publicity and bulletin committee of the National Secretaries Association.

"Dear Mrs. Johnson:

"I'm sorry it's taken me so long to respond to your invitation to describe my background and a typical day at work, but we have had a very busy legislative session during this last year of Governor Reagan's term in office. Since you indicated no deadline, I hope you can still use my answer.

"I was born May 4, 1938, in a small town in Austria and lived there with my parents and one brother until I graduated from a nearby business college. My father was an engineer in the local paper mill. Following graduation, I moved to the big city, Vienna, where I got my first job as a secretary in a manufacturing company.

1

"Adventuresome by nature, I was determined to see more of the world before settling down so I moved on after two years. I spent a summer in Sweden and a year in Germany before leaving for the United States where I planned to make my permanent home.

"The first few years I settled in Detroit, working my way up from a typist to an underwriter for a national insurance company. From there I made my move into politics by applying for a secretarial position at the American Medical Political Action Committee in Chicago. It was through that organization that I met Ronald Reagan. He was on the banquet circuit then and a speaker at one of our workshops. I was deeply impressed by the man and what he stood for. My decision was made. Should he decide to seek political office, as rumored, I would help in his election. When, soon afterwards, he announced his candidacy for governor of California, I quit my job and moved to San Francisco. While it took quite a bit of determination to accomplish what I had set out to do (I soon found out how naïve I was to think they were waiting for me!), I finally was successful in being hired by the Reagan for Governor Committee. I was, of course, the last person on the totem pole, but that didn't bother me as much as never seeing my candidate in person again!

"I had to wait until after the election when one of the governor's first appointees, Cabinet Assistant William P. Clark, Jr., asked me to come to Sacramento with him. This was my chance. I jumped at it and, as a consequence, can look back on the most rewarding eight years of my life. I never thought I would dread a change, but the impending one imposed on me by my boss's decision not to run for re-election is one I have yet to accept.

"Never have I enjoyed working more than on Governor Reagan's staff. My initial position in the Cabinet Unit was fascinating since my duties included taking minutes at the Cabinet meetings—where major administration decisions are made. When my boss became executive assistant to the governor, my job became more and more challenging and I became more intricately involved in our administration. Five years ago when the governor's personal secretary left, the coveted post was offered to me.

"You ask me to describe a typical day on my job. I'm afraid I will have to do it twice, for my day is totally different when the governor is *in* or *out* of the office.

2

"Contrary to situations I have known before, I look forward to every day I have the opportunity to work with and for the governor. He's a dream as a boss and possesses all qualities a secretary treasures—a pleasant personality, good sense of humor, the ability to delegate and make your job as challenging as you can handle and, as an extra bonus, never takes me for granted or demands what he can get through asking.

"The governor normally arrives at the office at nine (he's an avid reader and goes through at least five to six newspapers before leaving home), so I try to be in the office no later than 8:30 to get everything ready for him.

"I separate the mail, memos, and reports into three categories—signature, action, and information. If possible, I leave his schedule blank the first hour in the morning, giving him a chance to look through the material on his desk, dictate letters, or return phone calls from the previous day. It's usually the only informal time we have together to discuss projects, problems, or the appointments ahead. Once the meetings start, they are back-to-back the entire day and I have little chance to see him again.

"Personal accomplishments are difficult to achieve during business hours when the governor is in because I am busy handling the many incoming phone calls, screening the people who come and go, assuring a smooth flow of traffic into the 'inner-sanctum' and trying to keep the governor on time. The latter is a constant challenge because Ronald Reagan is no machine who adopts easily to rigid rules of ten to fifteen-minute appointments. Yet, the demands on his time are so great that there's no way to take this into consideration by allowing some leeway. The consequence, of course, is an often frustrated boss when I push him to conclude a meeting in the midst of a deep discussion. It's the hardest part of my job, but I have no choice—a problem can only be allocated so much time or another one goes unattended. Almost impossible are our efforts to pull him away from children and students. He loves young people and if he has a favorite audience it's the boys and girls who come with an array of questions, eager to hear his philosophy and to learn about government. If he has to leave them with hands still waving up in the air, anxious to be called, I can feel with him the frustration at having to end the meeting. Young people occupy a very special place in the governor's heart.

"Preparing the governor's schedule is nearly a full-time occupation itself. Easiest are the routine meetings. All I have to do is block out 'x' number of hours each month for cabinet meetings, staff work sessions, legislative matters, and news conferences, and inform the people involved. But all other requests for appointments, made by either the public or administration officials, take careful deliberation, research, and investigation, numerous phone calls, and often correspondence. Also, I have to be concerned about appropriate briefing memos for the governor, necessary security arrangements, and sufficient notice to the press if such coverage is desired. The many interruptions I face during the day are really not conducive to the concentration required to work out such a schedule in minute detail.

"Finally, at five o'clock, the governor's office is shut to visitors. If the governor does not have to rush off immediately to catch a plane or get ready for an evening event, we both work quietly at our desks about thirty feet apart for another couple of hours. That's when I review my assistant's work and the governor's dictation she transcribed which is ready for mailing upon my approval.

"The governor knows I'd never leave the office before him, but worrying about my getting home late and neglecting my husband, he will always try to get rid of me by assuring me that he no longer needs me. When his repeated urgings go unanswered, he will finally pack up and say, 'O.K., I shall finish up at home.' Sometimes we will then chat for awhile about current events or get into all types of philosophical discussions on issues or life in general. If I'm lucky he will end up telling me an inside story or a cute joke. That's always a special treat because no one can tell a story as he can.

"As hectic as days are with him in the office, I miss him when he's gone on a trip or attends out-of-the-office meetings. At the same time I rely on them or I would fall hopelessly behind in my correspondence. In just a few days, the letters I answer directly for the governor will have stacked up in the corner of my desk, but only during his absence can I attend to our citizens' many queries about our governor. You would be surprised how much correspondence has nothing whatever to do with the issues or government. He's a very popular man, an idol to many, and people want to know his opinions on anything from pornographic films to long hair; his secret for keeping so fit and trim or his favorite

4

foods. Many remember him as a movie star and ask for his advice in getting started or his help in finding a producer for a written play. Then, of course, there are countless worthy organizations seeking the governor's endorsement and membership, hoping their cause will be boosted by his association. Requests for personal items to be used in auctions and displays are also plentiful and just the other day the governor told me that not only is he out of old socks, but he can't keep the new ones. The hundreds of yearly financial appeals from individuals, groups, and charities are, of course, the most difficult to handle, but even a man much wealthier than the governor couldn't possibly contribute to them all. However, true hardship cases the governor insists on reviewing personally and helping if he can. An array of dear and warming stories come to mind, but lack of space won't allow me to cite even a few.

"The correspondence is never dull for the subjects are seemingly endless. It certainly keeps me busy and up-to-date on my boss's vital statistics! In between I also work on special projects—for instance, I try to find representatives for the governor when he can't accept a speaking invitation, and attempt to keep abreast of the activities of the foreign consular corps stationed in California, which is another project assigned to me.

"Can you see why I'm happy as is, and not pleased to give up my job? Not only are my responsibilities filled with challenge and variety but I am working for a rare man who commands my total admiration after eight years of close association. In a time when so many hearts are filled with cynicism about government and public representatives, my own experiences have allowed me to maintain my idealism and total confidence in our future. There are men who deeply care and put the welfare of our country above personal ambitions, not lacking the courage to stand up for the principles in which they believe. There is a difference between a compromise and a deal—how lucky I am to know the distinction.

"I married a countryman after becoming personal secretary to the governor. My husband, Chris, knows how important my job is to me and is very understanding if I work late, travel or talk excessively in the evenings about my day. We are outdoor people and weekends belong to us. We ski in winter and spend our summers boating and playing tennis.

"We have no children."

5

A Long Way from Home

There are a few fortunate people who have been privileged to work closely with Ronald Reagan over a period of time. I am one of those lucky ones. I have been his personal secretary for more than six years. With this background it is my pleasure indeed to write a book about this unusual man.

But whatever I might say about him would be colored by my own deep admiration of him and, therefore, the truths about him that I would write would be suspect.

But Ronald Reagan's character, his warmth, his wisdom, and his philosophy of life all shine through the letters he writes to friends, to relatives, to other national leaders, and to strangers who have corresponded with him.

He is a man who feels personally obligated to answer the appeals, requests, and compliments as well as the criticisms and differences of opinion that flooded his office since the first day he became governor of California.

With his permission I have singled out some of those letters—letters that I believe help reveal the real Ronald Reagan.

The picture most people have of Ronald Reagan is of a tall, handsome, youthful-looking man, almost dapper in dress, urbane, witty, warm, yet somehow aloof. They remember him from his movies—there were fifty of them—from his television days, his spectacular television speech for Barry Goldwater in 1964, his own campaigning, and his days as governor of California. Oldtimers may recall him as Dutch Reagan from his radio sports-announcing days for station WHO in Des Moines, Iowa.

There is a glamour in all of this—radio, movies, television, and high-level politics. But there is little in any of it that recalls the poor boy from small-town Illinois, the summertime lifeguard who over a seven-year span rescued seventy-eight persons from drowning, or the rugged running guard at tiny Eureka College in rural Illinois.

But Ronald Reagan's background and the environment in which he grew up come through again and again to those who have worked with him. These roots have had a strong and lasting effect on Reagan the man and Reagan the husband and father, as well as Reagan the politician, the governor, and the zealous defender of the American dream.

Ronald Wilson Reagan was born in Tampico, Illinois, but grew up largely in nearby Dixon on the Rock River. His father was John Edward Reagan, a first-generation black Irishman who sold shoes for a living—not often very successfully and sometimes not too soberly. This latter weakness left its mark on his younger son, Ronald, who, though no teetotaller, has seldom been known to have more than two drinks in an evening. His mother was Nelle Wilson Reagan, who instilled in Ronald the love for drama that eventually led him to Hollywood.

Ronald (early nicknamed "Dutch" by his father) and his brother Neil, who was two years older, grew up living the semi-idyllic Tom Sawyerish life of the typical small-town boy before the strident advent of radio, television, and the freeway.

In his autobiography, *Where's the Rest of Me*, written in 1965, Reagan describes this life. But underneath his gentle reminiscences one can discern how deeply his life has been affected by his childhood.

His father, a sentimental Democrat who believed fervently in the rights of the working man, also believed that every man should stand on his own feet. He had no use for bigotry in any form, and refused to let his family see *Birth of a Nation* because it dealt favorably with the Ku Klux Klan, and also refused one time to stay in a hotel that did not admit Jews.

From his mother, who did dramatic readings as a hobby, Ronald inherited a love for drama which led him to participate in high school and college drama clubs and eventually took him to Hollywood. From her, also, he received the fundamentalist Christian beliefs that even today strongly mark his letters, his conversations, his speeches, and his actions.

After high school the young Ronald Reagan worked his way through Eureka College where he played football, captained the swimming team, participated in campus dramatics and worked on the yearbook.

Graduating deep in the depression days, he decided he wanted to become a radio sports announcer. In 1932 jobs did not come easily but young Reagan hitchhiked from town to town seeking any kind of job in a radio station. After several months he found one, surprisingly as a sports announcer, on a station in Davenport, Iowa. The career that was to take him all the way to the governorship of California—and perhaps farther—had begun.

Memories of childhood and youth stay with us all. But Ronald Reagan's memories have been sharpened by requests from many persons to recall bits and incidents from his younger days. Recently a letter arrived at the Reagan home asking him to relate "the best advice I ever got." The advice came shortly after he was graduated from Eureka. It started him on his career.

"For seven years," Ronald Reagan recalls, "my last three in high school and my college years, I worked my way each summer as a lifeguard at a beach on the Rock River in my home town in Dixon, Illinois. It was located out in a kind of natural forest park. There was a rustic lodge, and a small group of families came there every summer. Many of them were second generation in summering at the lodge. I taught their children to swim. Most of the men were pretty successful and many of them would speak to me about looking them up when I got out of college. They were sure they could find something for me.

"Then came the crash of '29 and the Great Depression. I graduated from college in '32 and returned for one last summer of lifeguarding. The men who said they would like to do something for me, now, had very real problems of their own. Anyone who did not live through the Great Depression can't have any understanding of what it was really like.

"One man, however, did say that if I could tell him what I wanted to do, and if it was in any one of several lines of work, he was sure that he had enough due bills out that he could get employment for me. At that time, of course, just a job, any kind of job, was almost a miracle. This man, however, insisted that I would have to tell him what line of work I wanted to get in, what particular field I felt I could have a future in. He said that was the answer he must have before he would go forward.

9

"Well, unlike so many of today's young people, and yet not unusual for that time, I had graduated from college still with no set idea in my mind of what course I should follow. In addition to athletics, my other great interest had been dramatics, and yet, living in the heart of Illinois—in those days never having been east of Chicago or west of the Mississippi River—one didn't go about saying, 'I would like to be an actor.' Radio was relatively new. Having played football, as well as other sports in high school and college, I finally mustered up the courage, under his prodding, to tell him that I would like to be a radio sports announcer.

"The field was relatively new, almost unexplored. I thought at least it was into the field of entertainment. Well, of course, I had named an occupation in which he had no connections and could do nothing for me. So then, he gave me that best advice. He said, 'Look, this is probably better. I could have gotten you a job, (and he named several lines), but those who gave you the job would have been doing *me* a favor, not you; and, therefore, they would have considered they had done their part by simply giving you work. Now,' he said, 'you've mentioned a field that is new, that has a future. You must go out and start knocking on doors. You may have to knock on a couple of hundred of them—any salesman does before he makes a sale. You simply go in and tell them that you will take any job, including sweeping out, in order to get inside the industry and you will take your chances on working up from there; all you ask is a chance to work at anything within the industry.' He continued, 'Some place along the line, you'll find a man, who, even in spite of this depression, realizes that the world is going on and that he must be investing in new people, young people, if he is to have a future in the industry.'

"He was absolutely right. I started out hitchhiking, with only a few dollars in my pocket, trying station after station, usually failing to mention that I wanted to be a sports announcer—just simply saying that I would like to get into the announcing end of the trade—I figured sports announcing was a higher ambition that would come later—but telling that I would do anything, take any job, to get started.

"Sure enough, after knocking on a lot of doors, I came into a station, spoke to an unforgettable man who was the program director, a man who had come to this country from

Scotland. This time, I mentioned sports, but otherwise my pitch was the same as it had been in all the others.

"This man gave me probably the most unusual audition that has ever been given. He put me in the studio all by myself, told me he'd be in another room where I couldn't see him, listening, and when the red light came on, I was to imagine a football game, broadcast it, and try to make him see it. Well, that is what I did—for about fifteen minutes. He walked back into the studio and told me to be there on the following Saturday—I was broadcasting a Big Ten game, the Iowa-Minnesota homecoming game.

"And that was the start of everything that has happened since. But the advice that led to that was the thing—that it isn't necessary to have pull, or to have someone get you a position. If you really have the faith, and will decide what it is you want to do, and then go out and knock on enough doors, you will find someone willing to gamble on even the most inexperienced person, as I was."

From his earliest days Ronald Reagan has struggled with the correct pronunciation of his name, as did his father before him. Although his family has always pronounced the name as if it were spelled "Raygan," Americans typically pronounce it "Reegan." Many people who have pronounced it "Reegan" feel that the governor himself changed the pronunciation to "Raygan" as an affectation and they look upon what they think is a change as being not quite honest. Even after his eight years as governor that feeling persists among some Californians, a number of whom have written him, accusing him not only of changing the pronunciation but also of such sins as dyeing his hair.

Here is an excerpt from a typical response by Governor "Raygan."

"My entire life and that of my family has been spent in a struggle to convince people that our name was pronounced Ragan. I was eight years old when I remember my father as we were moving into a new town, protesting that now he would have to start teaching another group of neighbors how to pronounce our name. Always everyone has tried to call it Reegan. Even though I had the opportunity on the air to sign off and pronounce my own name correctly, others insisted on the mispronunciation.

"You said you had an innate suspicion of someone who would change his name or dye his hair. I think if the oppor-

11

tunity would present itself, and you could have a close look, you would find not only is my name Reagan, but my hair is not dyed, and there is a salting of grey down the part to prove it."

Though people in public life often suppose the public knows all about them, the truth is that the public absorbs much misinformation from newspapers and other sources. On occasion the governor was constrained to set the record straight. The following is a letter to the editor of the *San Francisco Chronicle*, written in 1972 in response to a letter written about him by one Charles Goringe.

"Dear Sir:

"In the interest of perhaps saving you some future space in the letters-to-the-editors column may I (hopefully) set the record straight regarding my military service in World War II.

"For some time now I have watched the exchange of letters in your paper and been grateful to those who kindly wrote in my behalf. The others seemed to nurse a suspicion that my uniform was wardrobe from 'Western Costume Company' or that I laid claim to the Medal of Honor.

"The most recent letter from Charles Goringe of Redding had me commissioned a captain direct from civilian life serving under Col. Sam Greenwald (deceased), a Paramount news cameraman. Sam was a long-time friend and commanded a combat camera crew flying bombing and reconnaissance missions.

"One thing the letters have proven is that my book, *Where's The Rest of Me*, was not a best seller. That's strange too because it is the best book I've ever written—it is also the only book I've ever written. In it I devoted quite a few pages to my four years in the military and voluntarily made it clear that I never heard a shot fired in anger.

"Since you don't have a space for a synopsis let me briefly summarize. Prior to World War II, I was in the Army Reserve as a 2nd Lt. of Cavalry (horse cavalry that is, although I missed the battle of the Little Big Horn). I earned the commission in the usual manner, cheating only on the physical—my near-sightedness was below the acceptable standard. Prior to Pearl Harbor a routine physical without the help, this time, of a friendly examiner, reduced me to 'limited service' status. Following Pearl Harbor I was called to active duty and assigned to Ft. Mason. Later in the rapid

12

expansion of the Air Corps I was transferred (not at my request) to the newly established unit of the Air Corps set up to train combat camera crews, make training films, and photograph highly secret projects, which, as far as I know, may still be classified.

"This unit, 'The 1st Motion Picture Unit A.A.F.,' took over Hal Roach studios, a nearby academy, and an airfield. Most of our personnel was recruited and commissioned from the ranks of the studios and more than 75 percent were over age and physically ineligible for the draft. Frankly they did a good job and some of them must have been the highest priced K.P.'s in Army history.

"I ended my service when the war was over as a captain. The only effort I made in four years to influence my status in the service was a refusal to accept promotion to major.

"There were fourteen million Americans in uniform who didn't get overseas. I never knew one who wasn't conscious of the great inequity in the fortunes of war, aware completely and humbly of the debt we owe to those who did."

Mr. Goringe's letter as well as the governor's reply brought to the governor still another letter, this one from Sam Greenwald who protested that he was not yet dead.

Eureka College is a landmark in Ronald Reagan's life. When he attended in the late 1920s and early 1930s it had fewer than 300 students. Reagan got through by working part-time, working summers, and borrowing money, which he began repaying almost immediately upon graduation. He has been a member of Eureka's Board of Trustees, has donated generously to it through the years, has been awarded an honorary doctorate by it, and has participated almost as actively as an alumnus as he did when a student.

Here is an exchange of correspondence with Kip Hayden, editor of the *Pegasus*, the Eureka newspaper, who in 1974 sought a "Back in My Day" essay from the school's most famous graduate. In responding, the governor made it clear that he regrets not at all having attended a small school:

"In my job these past eight years I've been a part of bigtime education as a regent of the University of California—all nine campuses and more than 100,000 students. All I've seen since has convinced me if I had it to do over again, I'd still go to Eureka. Just being elbowed in a crowd as 27,000 students go milling between classes isn't necessarily where the action is.

13

"One thing about Eureka, you can't remain anonymous. Students in the big assembly-line diploma mills can spend four years admittedly getting a good education, but never stretching themselves outside of their chosen studies to discover if they could participate in a play, sing in the glee club, make a team, or serve in a campus elective office. In a small college everyone is needed and there is no place to hide. If you make it in Eureka it's because your fellow students know you—not because they don't. And if you can make it under those circumstances you can make it anywhere.

"You are having a unique experience that is getting harder and harder to find in academia. If we aren't very, very careful it may one day be impossible to find. Live this experience while you can; the memory will be most precious. And help preserve it for others yet to come."

The governor's letter brought a return from Hayden who responded in part: "To say the least, you have rejuvenated my faith in the politicians of our country. As I last time wrote your office with my first letter I was told by my peers that I was asking the impossible, to receive an answer to a letter sent to a politician, let alone the governor of California. And yet I did receive your letter and a remarkable one it was."

In another letter about Eureka, Reagan speaks briefly of the new practice of allowing boys to visit in the girls' dormitory. "I just wonder how long the girls are going to hold still for what must have seemed like a cute idea—the visitation rights—but now must get a little annoying when ... they get caught half-clothed in the corridors by some joker coming to see his girlfriend."

He goes on to mention that "the Eureka of my memory was during Prohibition, but there were the same whispered words at the fraternity house about where the booze was hidden."

A letter to a fellow alumnus notes that "not too much has changed" at Eureka, "but still there is something of the characteristic so common and so disturbing in all of our colleges. This generation seems to stand off with a kind of attitude of what are you going to do for me? You and I remember when we thought of the college as ours, and we involved ourselves in its problems. . . ."

And to a member of his fraternity, Tau Kappa Epsilon, he wrote, "As the years have gone by the memories I have of the four years spent in the Teke House seem to grow brighter and richer."

High school, too, holds memories that Ronald Reagan recalled in a letter to Suzy Clegg, editor of the *Scimitar* at Santana High School, Santee, California, in 1972.

". . . somehow the good memories outlast the others; for example, teachers who seemed to honestly want you to succeed and who taught you *how* to think, not *what* to think.

"I didn't study as much as I should have, and if I had it to do over I would. The extracurricular activities were a large part of my high-school life, and this I do not regret. There is much to be learned in exposing yourself to the challenges of participation. First of all, you sometimes surprise yourself with what you can do. For me athletics led the list, followed by dramatics, and last, school politics. Believe it or not I was also on the staff of the yearbook.

"In athletics, while I won letters in track and basketball, football was an all-consuming passion. It was more than a game, and most players today will admit to this. I'm glad I played and glad the game meant so much to me. There were sweet victories and heartbreaking defeats, and there were those long autumn afternoons of drill that went on into the twilight (no lights then).

"Suzy, youth is impatient and sometimes those four high-school years seem to stretch out and appear meaningless. There is an old truism that you get out of a thing only as much as you put in. If you'll permit me one line of advice—cherish these four years, participate in them to the utmost whether you are on the field or in the cheering section, selling ads in the yearbook or decorating for a party. You'll carry a treasure of memories for many years."

Letters to Ronald Reagan often strike nostalgic chords and he responds in kind:

"You hit a nostalgic note with me when you mentioned that it was raining and you had just finished planting, and you spoke of the thoughts you have when you're out riding the tractor. Before I became governor I had my televison work reduced to about one day a week, and spent the rest of the time on our ranch. It was a working ranch, I had one employee, and he and I did what had to be done. I know very well the peace and the satisfaction in sitting out on that tractor with nothing but your own thoughts and looking back every once in a while at the furrows you were turning in your

15

own soil. Those days seem a long way back now. I hope they're not gone forever. I think very often of them and look forward to the day when I can do it again."

One letter came in asking him for a recipe his mother might have used in his childhood. "My mother has been dead for a great many years," he responded, "and I can't really recall any particular recipe. You know, back in those dark depression days . . . there was little of fancy food in our house. As a matter of fact, one of my favorites was oatmeal meat. I thought it was a luxury. Looking back I realize it was an effort to stretch hamburger by mixing oatmeal with the hamburger and then putting it in a pan and cooking it as you would hamburgers, putting gravy on it."

He adds, "If prices keep going up, it could well turn out to be the number-one recipe for almost everyone."

Books played a vital part in Reagan's early years. To Mrs. Marjorie Fluor he wrote: "I'm one of those who remembers vividly the magic of a library. Thank heaven I learned of the exciting world to be found in books and that excitement remains. No one can be lonely who has a book for company."

But on the other hand he has found that one can be too busy to read as much as one wishes. To S. L. Chandler of the Press Club of San Francisco, he wrote in 1968, ". . . the plain truth is, I've discovered books are something a governor (at least a new governor) dreams about, hears about, and stacks by the bed where they remain unopened.

"I've been a voracious, and not particularly selective reader all my life, but now reports and memorandums leave no time for books—not even books about me."

In the same letter he said, "If one book had to be recommended or chosen for a life of exile on the proverbial island, I think the Bible would be the unquestioned choice. I know of no other book that could be read and reread and continue to be a challenge as could the Old and New Testaments.

"This, then, makes the Bible the answer to your question about a book affecting my life. I don't mean to pose as a Bible student, and perhaps it is only now in the last few years that I've recognized its effect on me. My mother was deeply religious, and my early upbringing included regular Sunday School attendance. I'm conscious now of the extent to which I was influenced by almost a kind of osmosis."

The letter also mentioned a book that as a boy he read and reread, called *Northern Trails*. It planted in him "a love of the outdoors—so deep it lasts to this day, which will come as something of a surprise to those *Chronicle* editorial writers who mistakenly think I plot the destruction of the redwoods."

In a letter to his former Sunday-school teacher in 1973 the governor admitted that his success sometimes seems unreal. "Every once in a while I pinch myself sitting opposite the head of state of one or other of the dozen nations we've visited, thinking this can't be 'Dutch' Reagan here. I should still be out on the dock at Lowell Park."

Show Business

When Ronald Reagan first announced his candidacy for governor, and even after his great election victory in 1966, you could hear the skeptics in both parties demean "that actor" who dared to enter politics. But why should acting be considered less serious or respectable than any other profession?

Ronald Reagan is not the first actor to rise to the governorship of a major state. John Davis Lodge, a silent screen star, became governor of Connecticut. Other actors who have held public office include George Murphy and Helen Gahagan Douglas.

Former California Governor Edmund G. Brown, Sr., in his race against Reagan in 1966 probably lost many thousands of votes when a political film his campaign produced showed him telling a little black child that "You know, it was an actor who shot Lincoln."

Unquestionably, show business is a more colorful, diversified industry than most. It is one in which creation of images is part of the business. But people who deal with illusion must also deal with reality and some can deal with both very well, as Reagan watchers have found out. The people in show business, of course, are as different in character and ability as in any other segment of our society: there are the good and the bad guys; the educated and intelligent as well as the dropouts and misfits.

I have always admired the governor for displaying nothing but pride in his former profession and calling himself fortunate for having known Hollywood during its Golden Era. He recalls incidents and people with great nostalgia and affection; his own ability and success with typical humility and frankness.

Illustrative of Reagan's deep devotion to what he always refers to as "my former profession" is a quote by the late Irvin S. Cobb, humorist, actor, columnist. Reagan quoted

18

Cobb in a letter to Dennis R. Warren of Sacramento. Though an inveterate stealer and rearranger of one-liners, Reagan is quick to give credit on things important. So he had no hesitancy in using Cobb to reflect his own feelings. In response to criticism of actors as being childish, Cobb wrote:

"If this be true, and if it also is true that when the curtain goes up on eternity all men must approach the gates bearing in their arms that which they have given in life, the people of show business will march in the procession carrying in their arms the pure pearl of tears, the gold of laughter, and the diamonds of stardust they spread on what might otherwise have been a rather dreary world. When at last all stand before the final stage door, I am sure the keeper will say, open, let my children in."

I can hear Ronald Reagan quoting these lines, and with a certain quiver in his voice. He is a sentimental man. But while he loves the film industry, he is not an apologist for it. And he has strong feelings about what has happened to it in recent years—the nudism, vulgarity, and pornography. He is disturbed by these things. In a letter to Lou Greenspan, executive director of the Producers Guild of America, he wrote:

"I think the industry itself has driven away a great many of its one-time constituency. I think people are tired of being embarrassed in front of their children by the new realism and I think our young people, our children, have been subverted by the current fare to where they would have to be dragged kicking and screaming in to see a picture with a G rating. Yet, the same young people, in great numbers, have discovered the old movies of the 'Golden Era' on the late television shows. While they don't realize it they have, at the same time, discovered those pictures with no four-letter words, no nude scenes, no blatant sex, no vulgarity were better theatre than today's realism. That probably brings up what is the worst sin of much of today's movie fare. It is lousy theatre.

"When did we ever get the idea that in reaching for realism we could put something on the screen that was as effective as the audience's imagination? You can't turn two people loose in bed and expect them to portray the rapture of a wedding night anywhere near as well as the audience will do it for themselves in their own imagination given just a stimulant.

"My other view is that the industry should start beating a path to Washington but not to go down the deadly road of subsidy because if you do, you'll wind up with a senior partner, headquartered in Washington.

"No, what Hollywood needs is to eliminate the court decree that separated production and exhibition. Hollywood should be allowed, like a candy store, to make the pictures in the backroom and sell them in the front. That selling can be both theatre and a form of pay television where the theatre becomes the living room—something it has already become, but for bargain-basement entertainment.

In 1971, Reagan described his feelings about Hollywood to Charles Martin:

"I came to Hollywood, a sports announcer by trade, filled with all the star-struck awe of one who had from childhood been entertained in the house of illusion—the neighborhood theatre. I never did get over being awe-struck at finding myself working with and among those familiar faces. What I remember most and what it seems to me is so lacking today is the warmth and generosity of those great stars of yesterday—their willingness to accept and include newcomers like me.

"I don't know much about modern drama schools, but they can't be better than those long hours on the set when a Pat O'Brien, a Jimmy Cagney, a Bette Davis, a Dick Powell, and a Humphrey Bogart dropped a hint here, a bit of business there, or told most entertainingly a show-business story—with a message—and beginners like me awoke one day to discover we had learned a trade.

"I'll always be grateful that I knew Hollywood in the 'Golden Era,' when it was big, brash, and confident; it could do anything and usually did. It was also the Hollywood that became Mt. Olympus for the world's theatrical skill and talent . . . an unincorporated community with a news dateline— 'Hollywood.' At the same time, it was a friendly neighborhood of great warmth where the great helped the less great. Also, there was pride in craftsmanship."

Reagan traced a little of his own Hollywood career in response to a letter asking him for help in locating some of the films in which he appeared for a Reagan Film Festival at Humboldt State College in California. He recognizes that all of his films were not classics. *Law and Order*, for instance, "turned out pretty bad." *Accidents Will Happen* was "just another 'B' picture . . . made prior to my own move into 'A' films."

In *Dark Victory* he had "a minor role and an unhappy experience of trying to fit myself to an interpretation dictated by the director and with which I was in disagreement and, frankly, unable to really meet what it was he had in mind."

International Squadron, like so many World War II films, "is hard to take after the emotionalism and the spirit of the times are taken away."

On the other hand, *Knute Rockne, All American* was a film that "marked the end of an era" for Reagan. "It really closed off all those rah rah, Joe College pictures, with the hero winning the big game, the girl, and the job all at once. From my standpoint, also, it was the part which every actor comes to at some time or other in life that marks the transition into stardom.

"This was where I graduated from the 'B' pictures into subsequent films like *Kings Row*, which has been rated by some as one of the ten best pictures of all time."

But as for *The Ultimate Weapon*, it "is unknown to me; I don't know what picture that could be. It's possible the title was changed for TV distribution."

Or it's possible that some pictures are just better forgotten. Another picture the governor always wanted to forget was his last one, *The Killers*. He made it as a favor to a friend and in it, for the only time in his movie career, he played the bad guy. "It was a mistake," he says, making it plain that in films as in real life he prefers to wear a white hat.

Although *Kings Row* remains his personal best film, Reagan has difficulty picking out his all-time favorite. He wrote in 1971 to Carol Ann Selhorn of New Jersey: "There have been moments back through the years when I could have answered immediately, but as I try to pick one that would come to my mind I realize the theatre reflects the changing world, and what was an all-time favorite in a particular period is superseded by another with the changing times."

However, he continues, "In this era of mixed-up movies reflecting a mixed-up world, *Patton* stands out as one of the great motion picture-making jobs of this or any other time. It is unhesitating in its reflection of the brutality of war, totally honest in its probing of a man, and does this with an excellent taste which permits without offense the blunt language of the title character. It says something which needs saying today—that there are things for which men must be willing to die."

His admiration of *Patton* is unstinting. To its producer, Frank McCarthy, he wrote:

"I told you once I would hate anyone who ever played that role other than myself. Now I hate George Scott for proving that no one in the world but him could ever have played the part.

"Frank, it is a magnificent piece of picture-making and it says some things that very much need saying today. I have been greatly disturbed for sometime over the pernicious and constant degrading of the military. This picture restored a great deal of balance. I don't know whether Patton would ever be the kind of man you'd want to take on a picnic, but I do thank God that when trouble came, there were men like him around. I'm really too full of the picture yet to make specific comments other than to say it has been many years since I have so completely lost myself in a picture and have actually forgotten, while viewing it, that it was a picture. It was so real.

"I have long been an opponent, as you know, of vulgarity, obscenity, and profanity on the screen as we are seeing it in so many pictures. On the other hand, I've never believed that I was a total square and have never been opposed to the use of anything absolutely essential to the telling of the story. It did not offend me in the slightest that you had Patton talking as Patton talked. In fact, before going, I gave the Skipper quite a lecture on the man and the history surrounding him, and then told him that he would be hearing this kind of language, which didn't make it right for him or me to use, but that this was a part of the man and his character. Therefore, we sat through the movie and I had no embarrassment whatsoever about the language. It definitely belonged.

"Once again, just know that all of us were tremendously entertained and impressed, and loved every minute of the picture. Thank you for a real contribution to our nation at this time. Nancy echos and seconds all of this."

Reagan has great feelings of warmth and camaraderie, admiration, and affection for the members of his former profession. After seeing Danny Thomas in a nightclub act he wrote to him: "You were just great and I marvelled anew at your ability to take us from the sublime to the laughable and back to the sublime. It was sheer entertainment statesmanship and made me very proud.

"May I also say your courage in closing as you did was

most heartwarming. I have felt for a long time that the people of our land are hungry for a return to things of the spirit. Not enough of us use our talents and our positions in testimony to God's goodness."

He reacted similarly to the film, *Kotch,* starring Jack Lemmon and Walter Matthau. To Lemmon he wrote: "A few days ago flying to Washington I was one of a group of airborne at about 39,000 feet who must have been the happiest humans on or above the earth. You and Walter Matthau were responsible for this. For a few hours we watched your picture, *Kotch.*

"Jack, it was a pure delight, and I resolved as I took off the headphones to write you and also Walter, which I am doing, to tell you what a great joy it was to see real pros at work. If ever there was a two-man tour de force, this was it. I'll be seeing it again, because I want Nancy to see it, although I've described every foot of film to her.

"Please don't take it easy—keep on working and doing jobs like this one. You are needed by a great many people."

He sent a copy of that letter to Matthau with an added paragraph that read: "I have to add, just for you, your portrayal of an elderly man was so great, so perfect, that I'm sure every actor had the same reaction I did, that little uncertain question in the mind, 'Could I ever do such a job?' I'm afraid for most of us the answer is no. It's been a long time since I hated to see a picture come to an end, but on this one I wanted you to keep right on going and visit the young lady, drop in on your son for Christmas, and I wanted to watch you do it all for as long as that airplane would stay up there."

Unable to attend a dinner honoring Jimmy Durante, he sent a letter which read, in part: "Jimmy, if giving people pleasure and the gift of laughter were measured in gold, you would have given away a billion dollars. A few in our business earn the distinction of being called a 'legend in their own time.' You are among that few. You never got laughs by hurting or embarrassing anyone, your humor had heart, warmth, and kindness. You are in more hearts than you will ever know. May the road rise beneath your feet and the wind be always at your back."

Time after time he is asked to comment on actors he has known. Without exception, his words are kindly and gracious. About Errol Flynn he wrote: "Sometimes I could get so mad at him I wanted to hit him over the head with a camera. At the same time I felt a great tragedy surrounded him. Physically he was a magnificent piece of machinery. He could have been a fantastic athlete in almost any sport. In acting, of course, this gave him grace in action beautiful to behold. He was one of the few in our profession who could truly take the romantic roles in the costume epics and look the part so believably. He had total audience acceptance. This became evident in his few attempts at straight roles in modern clothes. While he wanted to do this, I always felt he lost some inner confidence when he was without the trappings of the costume pictures.

"The sense of tragedy I mentioned was because with all this going for him he had no confidence in his acting ability. He was fearful of competition from others in his own pictures. The result was [that] many times he would try to get script alterations taking advantage of his star power and influence to lessen some other actor's part in the picture. This is the point at which you wanted to hit him over the head with a camera. He really could hold his own. He had a commanding presence on screen. If he had only known his own capacity he would have realized how much better his scenes and the picture could have been if he had allowed the rest of the cast to help play and build those scenes.

"Errol was one of the most instantly likeable people I have ever met. He had great charm. Somehow I feel the problems besetting him in his private life stemmed from the same insecurity he felt in his profession.

"I'm glad I knew him and glad I had the opportunity to be in two pictures with him. I only wish somehow someone had been able to show him how little he had to fear and how really great he could have become. There is no one in the business now quite like him."

He told of his admiration for Barbara Stanwyck in a letter to Miss Ella Smith, assistant professor of dramatic arts at the University of Connecticut: *"Cattle Queen of Montana* was the only picture I ever made with Barbara Stanwyck, although I have known her for many years. She is one of the best thought-of and most respected performers in all the industry.

"Working with her I discovered why. She is a pro. Her only intolerance is of those who won't take our profession seriously, and who come to work without their lines learned

24

or who are late and careless in their work. She is ready every day exactly on time, her lines learned perfectly for each day's shooting, prepared to undergo whatever has to be done to make the scene better for the audience who will eventually see the movie.

"In *Cattle Queen* for example, there is a scene where she is bathing in a mountain lake. The director was prepared to shoot this with a double because the temperature of the water was in the mid-forties. Naturally, the scene would not be as good if the camera had had to play far enough away for use of a double. She insisted on doing the scene herself. She is most helpful to other performers, sacrificing many times some personal advantage in the scene and throwing the scene to another when she thinks it will benefit the overall story.

"You asked about the S.A.G. [Screen Actors Guild] award. Nothing illustrates more her personality and attitude. Those who knew her were concerned that if she suspected she was getting an award she wouldn't be there, so they invited her to come down and present the award to me. She was standing offstage, fully expecting to come out and make the presentation of the first such award to me, when she heard me making the presentation to her."

Both Reagan and Boris Karloff were active in the Screen Actors Guild "back in those dark days after World War II when we met for so many long hours each day to try and keep the studios open in the face of the communist-inspired attempt through labor troubles to dominate the industry."

To an acquaintance seeking anecdotes for a book about Karloff, he wrote that "I have only the warmest memories of him," adding, "Boris was one of the warmest, kindest, most gentle human beings I have ever met, and at all times a perfect gentleman. He was modest and unassuming and, yet, in his quiet way, contributed so much in our deliberations. He had great, good common sense plus a sense of fairness typical of his great integrity. Nancy was on the board in those days and both of us held him in such great affection that love is the only word I can use to describe him.

"I left out one other descriptive word. When the stories would lead into banter and joking, he also had a most delightful sense of humor. I'm sorry I can't recall some specific incident that would be of use to you. I can only say that many a time I would find myself looking at him and wondering how this kindly man fell into the type-casting of monsters and villains. He was the complete opposite of the parts he played."

Though he did not know Audie Murphy well, he took the death of the famed World War II Medal of Honor winner and postwar actor hard. After Murphy's death in an airplane crash he wrote a letter to Mrs. Murphy, which like so many of his letters, reflects his strong faith in God. It read in part: "When tragedy strikes we inevitably ask why, and, of course, there is no answer. But of one thing I'm sure: our lives have a purpose known only to God, and God had a plan for Audie Murphy which was not completed with his magnificent wartime service.

"Perhaps the fulfillment of that purpose is yet to come in the lives of Audie's sons. If that is so, then you are a very great part of God's plan. I know this is a difficult time for young people to see heroism in any act associated with war, and that is too bad. Some men will go through life and never find themselves in a position where they are the only ones who can do the dirty job that has to be done. Some will face such a moment and fail. Some, like Audie, accept and do the dirty job because there is no one else there to do it, and they know in their hearts it must be done. Your sons should be aware, and no doubt are, of what not only a nation, but civilization itself owes to men like their father."

At Peace with the Press

Ronald Reagan is an expert in dealing with members of the news media. He is comfortable with them and I think one can safely say that with a few exceptions he is well liked by them.

Considering the press's function, I think it's impossible for any public official to have more than a mutually respectful relationship with the press. It is unfortunate, however, when that relationship deteriorates to prejudice or outright hostility on either side. With both having such distinct and different areas of responsibility to the public, theoretically, they should be able to work for the common good. That it doesn't always work out that way is due to a variety of reasons on both sides.

One of the more serious reasons is the decline of professionalism among some newsmen. No longer do many of them consider objectivity essential. Those who embrace the "new journalism" no longer seem willing to leave opinion to the columnists and editorial writers. These reporters prejudge events according to their prejudices, and their news stories reflect their failure to get all the facts. You don't have to be a politician to be upset if you find yourself the victim of sloppy reporting or misrepresentation, but those in public office seem all too often to be the chief victims.

On the other side of the coin, public officials too often expect confirmation and justification of their words and actions in the media, forgetting that the media's job is to question, to report, and to criticize if criticism is called for. There have been countless instances where the press has exposed deplorable situations which would otherwise have gone unnoticed and unremedied.

A case is that of the lone and courageous reporter for the *Sacramento Union* who disclosed the outrageous benefits California's legislators had voted themselves at taxpayer expense.

This reporter succeeded in arousing the public to such an extent that the legislature was forced to rescind its pork-barrel actions. This, of course, is just a small example of the benefits of a free press; no one will argue that it is not one of the foundations of our country's freedom.

But we can only rely on it if its members perform in the highest tradition of their profession. What happens if they don't report accurately or completely or honestly? What recourse does the public or the office holder have if they report some stories and not others?

I recently read that a major TV network devoted more reporting time to trivial matters than to our nation's defense system which has dangerously declined in recent years. Is that a responsible free press, deserving of our trust and confidence?

We must always be just a little suspicious of whatever we read. I have been witness to too many examples of inaccurate or biased reporting. And sadly, once the damage is done, no letter to the editor or retraction on some inside page of the paper can ever undo the damage or change the opinions created by one false headline or one misstatement of facts.

The governor touched on the press's ability to do harm in a letter to Maxwell H. Smith of Malibu, California: "I very much fear the press contributes to the divisiveness in our country by printing stories and ignoring their responsibility to check out the facts themselves. They justify this by saying, well, if some prominent individual makes a charge, that charge becomes news. But can they really absolve themselves from a responsibility as an information agency to editorially present the facts on the other side? Perhaps this is one reason why a great many American institutions are today so suspect."

Governor Ronald Reagan probably spent more time than he should have trying to set the record straight on such sensitive issues as education and mental health when his administration was victimized in the press. Unfortunately, his efforts seldom seem to have reached the public. Not surprisingly, press misrepresentation on personal matters also annoyed him.

In a letter to William F. Buckley, Jr. of *National Review*, he alluded to an exchange of published letters between Buckley and Abe Rosenthal, managing editor of the *New York Times*, letters in which Reagan said Rosenthal made factual errors. The letter reads:

"I was cleaning a few stacks of correspondence away on my desk, and came upon your letters to Mr. Rosenthal of the *Times* and his letter to you. I had kept all this because I enjoy reading Buckley—Mr. Rosenthal I can take or leave alone.

"Looking at his letter again, however, I realize he shot a few arrows into the air, and you had never been provided (by me) with a tracking device to determine how far off course his little arrows were.

"Arrow number one had to do with our residence and the old 'mansion.' He says Nancy declared it a fire trap and moved out, and wealthy friends bought a house which we rented at twelve hundred dollars per month. At the end of a year the state kindly took it over; thus rent now becomes income. All because we could not go back to living in the 'old mansion.'

"The state fire marshal declared the 'old mansion' a firetrap long before we moved in. We moved out after a fire scare which served to remind us we had an eight-year-old nesting about thirty feet above the ground. Wealthy friends did not immediately buy a house for us to rent. We rented from a native Sacramentan, who subsequently put the house up for sale at the request of the Internal Revenue Service, who had him on the cuff for about half a million in unpaid taxes. We searched the town for another house to rent, and were within two weeks of being evicted as our unsuccessful search went on.

"It was at this point a group of citizens (some friends and some men we'd never met who are stalwart Democrats) bought the house and took over the lease. We continued paying the rent for about three years. As the 1970 election drew near, my opponent began a campaign of innuendos that, somehow, by paying my own rent, I was beholden to 'half-hidden millionaires' who were my landlords. The California Constitution requires the state to provide a governor's residence. The 'old mansion' has long since been taken over by Parks and Recreation, and it is a tourist attraction. Please note, tourists are not allowed above the ground floor, due to the fire hazard. So a year ago I told the legislature I was fed up with all the hanky-panky, and the state could damn well take over paying the rent, thereby severing any supposed umbilical cord between me and the landlords."

 In the same letter Reagan unhesitatingly lashes a *Times* article on his tax troubles. He goes on, "Now since the *Times* saw fit to pursue my tax matter—all the way to having someone pose as a cattle buyer visiting ranches and sniffing around for a Reagan brand, all of which resulted in a *Times* Sunday feature as dishonest as the *Times* could make it—I'll spoil his martini with a fact or two.

"My continuing interest in cattle and ranching did not produce the tax shelter his paper alleged. My total investment in breeding bulls was ten thousand dollars, which doesn't buy many cattle at today's prices. I regularly receive ordinary income from that investment which I dutifully declare.

"The mystery of my evil loopholes is somewhat reduced when you consider that two very legitimate items alone, namely 'other taxes' (deductible for purposes of computing income tax under California and federal laws) and contributions to church and charity, totaled almost half my gross salary as governor.

"By the way, 'when the roll is called up yonder,' do you think not paying a tax you don't owe will rate as many demerits as receiving stolen property and selling it for profit? Maybe that is oversimplification, but somehow in my mind it applies to the *Times* and the purloined [Pentagon] papers."

Misinformation released by the media often resulted in a flood of letters to the governor either criticizing him or asking him to explain. The tax story triggered one such flood since many newspaper stories never made it clear that he had not evaded his state taxes; he merely did not owe any. Some liberal newspapers editorialized against him, implying that he had evaded his taxes and should have paid something.

Ignored by most of the press was the principle of tax paying laid down by the famed liberal judge, Learned Hand. Hand wrote that "there is nothing sinister in so arranging one's affairs as to keep taxes just as low as possible. Nobody owes any public duty to pay more than the law demands. Taxes are enforced exactions, not voluntary contributions. To demand more in the name of morals is mere cant."

In a letter about his taxes and misrepresentation of the situation not only in the press but in the classroom, Reagan explained: "I cannot tell you how much I appreciate your writing to me and giving me a chance to hopefully straighten the record on the misinformation you received in the classroom.

"Your story is not an unfamiliar one. I have come to the conclusion that much of the dissatisfaction, the mistrust of all our established institutions, is being fostered in too many social studies courses.

"As you perhaps know, through all my years in pictures I had as a sideline, in fact a sideline which was my main interest, ranching. It was a small operation, breeding horses and raising some cattle, and certainly I never could have lived on the basis of my success as a rancher. I was unable to continue actively in that sideline activity when I became governor. Disposing of the ranch, but wanting to at least have a feeling of still being active in agriculture, I invested a relatively small amount of money in breeding bulls through a company which handles the business end of putting those bulls out on lease on a number of ranches throughout the country. Last year, when the furor arose over the fact that last year I had no state income tax obligation, the *New York Times* went out of its way to publish the fact that I had this cattle investment. They made it seem as if it was a tremendous, Texas-size, operation, and then falsely stated that it was a tax device and probably the reason I had no income tax obligation. They charged the old demagogic thing of some kind of loophole. The truth is, my modest investment of a few thousand dollars in a small herd of bulls actually contributed a few dollars of income I had to declare. I had a small profit, less than a few hundred dollars over and above the expense of keeping the bulls.

"Since this whole thing was tied into the matter of my state income tax, perhaps I should give you in advance some information on that. First of all, this was the first time such a thing had ever happened to me, and it was purely the result of my transition from the television industry which, obviously, paid several times more than does the job of governor. Naturally, there were many things I could not shift immediately, responsibilities to charities I had previously supported, etc., in those first few years in office, so my tax situation was rather up and down. For example, the year before I had no tax obligation to the state, my income tax was more than double my total salary as governor. I am sure the teacher would be happy to know that this year I have paid a normal state income tax.

"To sum up, you can inform this teacher that I have no subsidies from government of any kind. I own a small number of bulls; I board them out and pay their board at a variety of ranches and, at the end of the year, they deliver a few dollars in additional income."

The governor's embarrassment and anger at the rash of misleading stories on his tax situation were matched only by the embarrassment of the reporter who asked the question that brought the reply that, no, the governor had paid no state income tax for the year 1970.

Perhaps I should give a little background here. Income tax returns in California, like federal tax returns, are confidential. It is a felony for a state employee to divulge them. Yet one state employee who saw the governor's tax returns passed the word to a college radio-station reporter that the governor had paid no taxes.

The script of the college reporter's almost unnoticed broadcast was then passed to the members of the Sacramento press corps. The person who asked the question of the governor, a careful and accurate reporter, was dismayed at the outcry that resulted. He wrote to the governor: "The stories that resulted—like so many—[were] blown all out of proportion. A curiosity item dwelling upon vindictive reaction to your own personal financial misfortune—trivia when compared to the problems of the state and the suggested solutions.

"For my part, for your embarrassment I am truly sorrowful. For the personal difficulty it has caused you I shall be eternally sorry."

Reagan responded: "Nancy and I were both happy to receive your letter and want you to know we had already been informed that you were not the plant who was supposed to ask the question.

"We understood your motive in asking. Don't feel bad about it because someone else would have asked, and probably with the same result.

"Have no fear with regard to our friendship: we still value it very highly."

Reagan also responded to what probably is a classic story of how inaccuracies printed and reprinted by the press become conventional truths in the eyes of both the press and the public when a generally respected capitol reporter started a story that began, "With Spiro T. Agnew gone from the public scene, Governor Reagan has emerged as perhaps the nation's most controversial figure of speech." He recounted some Reagan "bloopers" without putting them in the context of the time, place, and situation where they were said. More in an effort to set the record straight than in anger, Reagan wrote the following letter to him.

"I couldn't help but drop you a note regarding your recent story in the Sunday *Sacramento Union*. You know I'm not given to railing at the press but in this instance I do feel justified in pointing out that the overall effect your story gives of putting my foot in my mouth is based less on what I've said than on what someone else has accused me of saying.

"I'm sure you are not guilty of deliberate distortion but have only accepted the oft-repeated version of the incidents you used as gospel. If so, it is a case of journalism feeding on original journalistic errors.

"Sometimes I'm reminded of all the Jimmy Cagney imitators who inevitably wind up saying in Cagney style, 'you dirty rat,' until everyone believes that is a classic line from one of his movies. The truth is, Jimmy never spoke the line in his entire life.

"Let's take my supposed use of the term 'blood bath.' Yes, I used the words but not in the way one, and I emphasize, *one* reporter carried them. Others of the press covering the meeting found no news in the statement nor was there any until one reporter put the words in a context completely different from the way they were used.

"Officials of the University of California who are not usually hesitant to criticize me were present at the meeting and were high in their approval of what I'd said. Perhaps (as I've said since) a more apt figure of speech might have been, 'bite the bullet.' At any rate, 'blood bath' was *never* used in the sense of encouraging violence on the campus in those troubled times—actually the very opposite was intended.

"You did correct the wording of the 'redwood' line but still used it as an illustration of a political slip of the tongue. Frankly, I'd use it again because I was talking about the pride Californians should feel about the way we have saved our redwood trees. It certainly was not a remark indicating callous disregard for the redwoods. But again, one reporter reinterpreted and my opponent in the campaign took off with it.

"As for the most recent remark and the one which evidently prompted your story—you know how careful I've been to avoid any statement that might endanger Patty Hearst.

33

How many private conversations have you been in where speculation, theorizing, and even outright cracks have been made, none of which you would make public in a news story? Possibly I'm denied that right, but I can't help but feel that (again) the *one* reporter who heard of my remark secondhand and *made* a story of it was guilty of an even greater irresponsibility. And frankly, my attempt to level with all of you in the press corps was used by many in a way that revealed a total lack of concern for Patty's safety.

" 'No comment' is becoming a more attractive refuge every day but I'd hate to use it because it would be of little benefit to the people of California.

"I hope you accept this in the way it is intended. It was written only because we have had a relationship I value."

The reporter responded, "I appreciate your note of March 14 and the thought that went into it.

"There certainly was no attempt to deliberately distort your comments. Our credibility, both with news sources and with our public readership, is vital to the survival of a free press.

"Yes, statements once reported—regardless of degree of accuracy and context—sometimes become etched in granite. It is the duty of a professional, fair-minded reporter to make certain the basic facts were accurate, as well as providing a complete frame of reference for those facts."

On a lighter note he promised "never to write that *Bedtime for Bonzo* was the pinnacle of your screen career."

The governor's letters in seeking to set the record straight often referred to the *New York Times* which, while it may run "all the news that's fit to print" does not always do so accurately. In one case a Connecticut teacher wrote the governor because "my students have asked me to write to you about the enclosed article from the *New York Times*." The article dealt with remarks the governor had made concerning those involved in Watergate. Though it ran in the *Times* the article was filed out of Sacramento by United Press International (UPI). The first two paragraphs read, "Governor Ronald Reagan said yesterday that the Watergate spies should not be considered criminals because they are not criminals at heart.

"Mr. Reagan, who espouses a strict law-and-order philosophy, conceded that the electronic bugging of the Democratic party headquarters was illegal but said 'criminal' was too harsh a term to use."

The teacher wrote of his students: "They are confused. Briefly, what they want to know is: If a poor man breaks into a supermarket and steals food to feed his family, is he a 'criminal' or is he an 'illegal'? If a businessman hires someone to break into his competitor's office and steal a secret process, is he a 'criminal' or an 'illegal'? If a politician hires someone to break into his opponent's office to steal information that will help elect him and his associates into offices worth millions of dollars, is he a 'criminal' or an 'illegal'?

"Ordinarily I would not have paid too much attention to these queries. But, 1) I can't answer them; and 2) these children are the sons and daughters of American executives and government officials who will inherit the sort of job that you have. They are mostly Republicans and they want an explanation. I believe they have a point. I hope you will give them a personal and responsive answer."

Reagan's reply: "I am delighted to have the opportunity to answer your students' questions and congratulate them for their perception and their concern.

"Part of my happiness in answering is because it gives me a chance to point out the distortions which have become so commonplace in recent years in press coverage particularly where public figures are concerned. In the case of the *New York Times* story the distortion is one of omission and slanting to get exactly the tone that prompted you to write.

"I realize the press cannot devote unlimited space to carry, for example, a rather lengthy conversation (which this was) but it is nevertheless improper to alter the gist of that conversation so as to provide a headline, 'Reagan says spies are not criminals.'

"Of course the breaking and entering of the Watergate headquarters was both a criminal act and an illegal act. The hypothetical case of the poor man stealing food for his family was likewise criminal and illegal. In our system of justice allowance is made, however, for extenuating circumstances. Any court would deal differently in the case of the poor man stealing food and the businessman attempting to steal business secrets for personal gain.

"In my conversation with the reporters I had remarked about the great human tragedy involved in Watergate; that campaign tactics have for many years had a kind of 'fraternity initiation' atmosphere where both sides expect

35

shenanigans. In this context I pointed out that none of the men had criminal natures and probably wouldn't ever intentionally double park, but now their lives could very well be ruined and a number will undoubtedly go to prison for something done in the emotionalism of a political campaign, and which none of them thought of as criminal. Do college students think of themselves as criminals when they go from one campus to another to steal a statue or historic bell prior to the big game? But they are stealing.

"In my conversation I made it clear the guilty should be punished, and I expressed a hope that possibly we'd all review our attitude toward campaign hooliganism in the future. I do take issue with you that offices are sought because they are worth millions of dollars. If monetary gain were the reason, then I would have stayed in TV where I was earning roughly five times my present salary as governor.

"But referring back to campaign hooliganism [may I remind you that] Senator McGovern stated publicly he knew Watergate was a Republican caper because his informant in the Nixon headquarters told him it was. In Kansas, according to a news story, his staff happily boasted of breaking and entering to get party membership lists they weren't supposed to have during the primary. Ellsberg, now freed on a technicality, confessed to stealing the Pentagon papers because he felt the end justified the means. Columnist Jack Anderson printed transcripts from the grand jury and refused to identify his source, although taking such transcripts is a felony. Ralph Nader has urged industrial employees to steal and to provide him with information from their employers' files.

"All of these things are wrong. All are technically criminal and illegal. How many of us in hearing them mentally made allowance for some or all? But the truth is, Watergate can't be wrong and Ellsberg right.

"There is a great need for all of us to stop short, take inventory, and see if we don't need a return to the ethics of an earlier day when personal honor enjoyed a higher status than we've been giving it. We can have human compassion for those who slip, but we can also demand personal accountability.

"What has been happening to our society has been a gradual and insidious thing. It includes, if you will, our acceptance of the intentional foul in basketball. If an opponent by good playing has moved into position for a sure shot is it right to foul him and rob him of the reward he's entitled to?

"Watergate will serve a useful purpose if all of us will decide that law and order begins with each one of us."

One of the early controversies of the Reagan administration was the firing by the Board of Regents of the University of California of University President Clark Kerr. This was in February, 1967.

Additionally there was ongoing controversy between Governor Reagan and the university for almost the entire eight years of his governorship. In March of 1972 the governor wrote to the editor of the UCLA *Daily Bruin* in an effort to correct statements and innuendoes Kerr made in an interview with a *Daily Bruin* reporter.

"In your March 1 issue, you carried a story by one of your staff writers, Dave McNary, containing an interview with former U.C. President Clark Kerr. I'm sure Mr. McNary wrote in good faith and with complete confidence in the answers provided by Dr. Kerr. My letter is prompted by the rewriting of history which took place in that article and which gave at least a chilling reminder of *1984*.

"First of all, to refer to the campus turmoil between 1964 and 1967 as 'peaceful nonviolent affairs' is like calling the Johnstown Flood a backed-up drain. All through the 1965 gubernatorial campaign, wherever my opponent or I appeared, the people had one thing uppermost in their minds: the question would be shouted in chorus, 'What are you going to do about Berkeley?' Neither Governor Brown nor I could seek this job without recognizing something had to be done.

"The clear impression is given by Dr. Kerr that I succeeded in firing him at the first regents' meeting I attended three weeks after my inauguration. It is time the truth is put on record. At my first regents' meeting, routine business was conducted for some hours. When we went into executive session late in the afternoon, I wasn't aware that two of the regents and Clark Kerr were not in their places until the two regents returned, visibly upset. They announced that Dr. Kerr had called them into his office to deliver an ultimatum. He told them he was aware of the two years of strained relations with the board and he could not continue under such circum-

37

stances; therefore, he demanded a vote of confidence from the board—that day—or he would resign. One regent said that perhaps the board should give in because to do otherwise might be embarrassing to me. Until then, I hadn't participated in any of the board's discussions, but now I told them they had no right to make a decision involving the university based on its possible effect in Sacramento. They should do what they believed was best for the university. On a roll-call vote, the ultimatum was rejected.

"As for the rest of the rewritten history, Angela Davis, after public declaration that she was not just a communist in the sense of subscribing to that philosophy but was a member of the American Communist Party, was ordered dismissed. The regents had no choice . . . the university itself had a rule on the books that no one could be hired to teach who was a member of that party *or any other organization* whose tenets restricted freedom of thought. A court order cancelled the dismissal, but the university told us she had been hired for one year only and would not be rehired when the year was up.

"One last thing: budgets. The university administration has used the phrase 'budget cuts' over and over again until, like 'newspeak,' there is widespread belief that we did indeed reduce existing budgets. This is patently false. During my administration, enrollment at the university had increased 35.4 percent; state financial support for the university had increased 56.8 percent. That should answer two more discrepancies—one, that the university has quit growing and, two, that we have reduced support.

"May I take the liberty of suggesting that you of the *Daily Bruin* have a great opportunity to advance the cause of truth. Don't believe what you are told without checking to see if there is another side—and that goes for what I've just written. Check me out."

Many of the governor's letters to members of the press were meant not only to set the record straight but also to inform and educate. A letter to a California columnist on the complicated subject of tax reform provides a good example.

"I read with great interest your column (May 19), 'We Can't Stand More Tax Relief.' As you can imagine, I'm not in agreement with a number of your conclusions.

"It is true that our tax reform proposal this time and for the first time contains an increase over and above the shift of property tax to other tax sources. However, that increase is not a 'slick' way of augmenting the state's take from the taxpayer. The increase is earmarked for public schools and represents a necessary response to the Serrano opinion of the Supreme Court.

"Another element of our proposal, the increase of the 'automobile in-lieu tax' goes entirely to city, county, and local schools in equal shares. This was done to compensate in part for our insistence that property taxes, once reduced, remain frozen at that level.

"In your comparison of our proposal with the Moretti plan you suggested that ours was a greater burden to the 'little guy.' Since his plan raises income taxes eight hundred million dollars and ours reduces them slightly and his plan includes an actual net tax increase more than five times as great as ours, I have to disagree with your conclusion.

"Finally you say, 'The fact remains the state is short of the money it wants and the taxpayers are going to come up with it somehow.' In the last five and one-half years, the state has returned directly to the taxpayers more than two billion dollars. There was the one-time ten percent rebate on income tax, the twenty percent rebate this year, the seventy-dollar rebate to homeowners a few years ago and the seven hundred and fifty-dollar property-tax exemption. The state pays local government several hundred million dollars each year to make up for this reduction in local property tax revenue.

"Incidentally, while our proposal contains a certain amount of new money for schools, if federal revenue sharing is adopted, we will be able to offer the taxpayers an across-the-board cut in state income taxes at the same time we increase state aid for schools.

"Most of the increase in the state budget is in the two-thirds of the budget which is returned to local government. We actually run the state, including the University of California and the state colleges plus highway construction and all the other state functions, on one-third of the total state budget. And we have fewer employees than we had five years ago. Of the citizen's tax dollar, running the state takes less than seven cents. The federal government takes about sixty-five cents and local government and schools use thirty cents. If real savings are to be made for the taxpayer, they can be made by citizens paying closer attention to how their money is spent in their own communities and by Uncle Sam in Washington. If the state closed down our great universities and colleges entirely the taxpayer would only get a reduction of less than one and one-half cents on the dollar. May I suggest there are better pickings for the taxpayer than Sacramento.

"Someday, why don't you pay us a visit and let us lay out the whole complicated matter for you? Frankly, we think there is money to be saved in government and you could be of help."

A letter to Brigadier General James F. Hamlet, commander of the First Cavalry Division's Third Brigade, alludes to what Reagan, along with many other Americans, thought was biased television coverage of the war in Vietnam:

"Dear General Hamlet:

"Some time ago you evidently challenged a CBS correspondent to go with you in your helicopter to visit the Third Brigade, First Cavalry Division, where they were engaged with the enemy. Recently the film taken of this visit was played here in the states on CBS News. May I say it was a most refreshing change from the usual CBS war coverage. I couldn't help but write and tell you how very proud you made a great many of us. Your remarks in your interview and the remarks of your men made us realize how deeply indebted we are to people like you who are doing so much in behalf of freedom for all of us."

The governor's older daughter, Maureen, has also felt the slings and arrows of an inaccurate press. Maureen complained in a letter to the editor of the *San Diego Union,* a copy of which she sent to her father, that "your newspaper printed an account" of a speech she had given "which is a complete distortion of my views. . . ."

Her father responded in a philosophical vein: "Based on my own experience I wouldn't suggest you hold your breath until you get the retraction or apology." He added, "If it will help any, let me just say that I'm sure you are overly concerned about how many might see it and possibly be offended. They'll probably never see it. I am amazed at how little most people do read the papers or even remember the stories. I know we all assume that, because it's there and because we saw it, everyone has read it. But I'm afraid most people scan the headlines, turn to the stock report, the sport page, or the comics, and that's it. So don't lose any sleep over what happened."

An Eye on the Horizon

I feel sorry for any man occupying a governor's chair without holding his own deep-seated personal philosophy. For every governor is faced with a multitude of grave problems, each of which seems to have legitimate and persuasive arguments for and against each possible solution. These are presented forcefully, and often directly, to the governor, by the proponents and opponents of each issue, including legislators, lobbyists, special interest groups, and news media.

Under this barrage where does the sincere, honest chief executive find his answer if not within himself? When the temptation to make a political decision, instead of going with the right decision regardless of politics, becomes ever so attractive, as it sometimes does, strength of character, supported by strong personal convictions and ideals is desperately needed.

The decision-making process varies from administration to administration. I have been told that former Governor Edmund G. (Pat) Brown did not have a hard and fast system. He left it up to his department heads to come to him with problems they couldn't solve. Brown had about forty department heads reporting directly to him.

Our administration was never a rudderless ship. Shortly after entering office, Ronald Reagan established the semiweekly cabinet sessions as the vehicle he would use to keep abreast of the state's problems. Attending these meetings were the four agency administrators, the director of finance, the republican constitutional officers as well as his own top-level staff.

In California the statewide constitutional officers are the governor, the lieutenant governor, the secretary of state, the controller, the treasurer, the attorney general, and the superintendent of public instruction. During Reagan's first term all but the attorney general were Republicans. In his second term all were Republicans except the secretary of state and the superintendent of public instruction.

Governor Reagan reorganized the government within weeks after his swearing in. He set up four cabinet-level agencies, each headed by a secretary. These were the secretaries of Business and Transportation, Agriculture and Services, Resources, and Health and Welfare.

The cabinet meeting format resembled board of directors meetings in that every issue was "round-tabled" and everyone had his say. The major difference was that there was no vote taken at the end. It was the governor alone who made the final decision on each issue, based, of course, on all the information he had received.

Obviously, not all problems could be settled with one discussion. Some issues were discussed in as many as thirty or forty meetings. On other occasions the governor would request a period for quiet contemplation. He would take the problem home and do his soul-searching at night. Whatever the outcome, it was always the result of his convictions, backed by the courage to carry out what he felt was right.

That courage was renewed constantly by the governor's strong faith in the Lord. In a letter to an old friend, the Reverend Ben H. Cleaver of Cape Girardeau, Mo., in May of 1971, he wrote,

"I am very grateful today for a faith in which you played a part in instilling within me. The Lord sometimes must tire of hearing me ask Him for strength, courage, and wisdom. I couldn't attempt this job for one day without His help."

The letter was one expressing general frustration with both the legislature and the bureaucracy. Of the legislature he wrote, "We are into what should be the closing weeks of the session with absolutely nothing accomplished. Fortunately, in their obstructionism and hostility, they have made serious political mistakes. . . .

"Now they are attempting to hold up legislation and the budget until they can force me to join them in announcing the need for a tax increase because they realize they've put themselves in an untenable position with the public. . . .

"If I have to admit to the need for tax increase, I will only do so because, having secured welfare reform and having reduced the budget as far as is humanly possible, the revenues are still insufficient and are needed to avoid deficit. I absolutely refuse to support a tax increase for new or additional spending."

Returning to welfare reform, he wrote that "about a year

43

ago I appointed a task force, including citizens from the community as well as people in government, to review the entire ridiculous welfare structure. I think we are the only state that has finally compiled the information we have and most of my fellow governors are coming to us for that information."

Then he turned to his dealings with the bureaucracy. "I have kicked the bureaucracy in the shins, and I am discovering how great can be their resentment. They have a very tight union. There occurs even sabotage within our own state government from those in the permanent structure who think elected representatives are only temporary and, therefore, to be ignored. I understand better the meaning of the poignant lines written by Whitaker Chambers when he turned away from communism. He said, 'When I took up my little bow and aimed at communism, I also hit something else. What I hit was that socialist revolution which, under the name of liberalism, has been inching its ice cap over the world and this nation for the past twenty years. I knew of its existence, but I was totally unprepared for its extent, the depth of its revolutionary anger.' "

Tax problems, in all their ramifications, were always present during the Reagan years in Sacramento. Despite never-ending efforts to "squeeze, cut, and trim" every possible ounce of fat out of state government, inflation, federally mandated programs, special needs, and efforts to limit local property taxes drove state spending up every year.

Glib spenders early called on the governor to institute a withholding program for state income-tax collections similar to the federal government's withholding program as a way of easing the burden. They said the program would not only bring in extra money but would also help the state's chronic cash flow problem.

The governor held out as long as he could, proclaiming that "my feet are in concrete" on the issue of withholding. His philosophy was that withholding made taxes too easy to pay because people didn't miss money taken out of their paychecks. "Taxes should hurt" he said, so that taxpayers would be *aware* of them and pressure their legislators to hold taxes down.

The phrase "taxes should hurt" came back to haunt Governor Reagan many times as editorial writers, columnists, and others deliberately twisted the remark to mean that he was heartless and cruel, and didn't care if people had to scrimp to pay their taxes. That, of course, wasn't—and isn't—the case at all. Few governors have cared as much for all the people and none has worked as hard as Ronald Reagan to keep taxes under control.

In a letter to Caspar Weinberger, then chairman of the Federal Trade Commission, but previously the state finance director, the governor explained that, "The deciding factor, however, had nothing to do with that, nor have I changed my mind about the philosophy back of the system, but the increase in the income tax wouldn't solve our cash-flow problem which is getting very acute. I just saw no other way out. Some of our hard-nosed friends are, of course, very resentful. However, one plus is that our most recent surveys and the polls we've been quietly taking, as you know, reveal that beginning last May, there was a strange shift in sentiment and the majority was for withholding. My own interpretation is that probably last April was the first time people felt the full impact of the '67 tax increase, and I've had individuals contact me who agree with me philosophically but who have said they need the convenience that it offers. Several legislators have come to me and told me that their districts previously against have, by way of polls in their newsletters, undergone the same change.

"The tremors from the cracking of concrete around my feet must have been felt in Washington."

The mention of cracking concrete referred to his earlier statement that his feet were in concrete. When he announced to the press his decision to endorse withholding he did it with the jocular remark that "That sound you hear is the concrete cracking around my feet." Later, members of the press, as a gag, presented him with a slab of concrete with two solid footprints imbedded in it.

In another letter he made it clear the decision had not been an easy one. "Next time I see you, I'll show you the nail holes in my hands," he wrote, adding, "I spent a few sleepless nights but as hard as we tried we could find no long-range solution other than this one. I still think the federal government perpetrated a crime on the people when it first spawned this, but the crime is almost a catching disease and, eventually, states like ours find no alternative."

A federal program that caused no end of problems for the Reagan administration was the Office of Economic Opportunity, also known as the War on Poverty, and especially one

45

of its offspring, known as Rural Legal Assistance. The governor concluded that RLA lawyers were more interested in disrupting the orderly administration of the state for ideological reasons than they were in helping poor people with their legal problems.

Consequently, in January of 1971, as was his right under the law, he vetoed the OEO grant to RLA that would have allowed it to continue operating. A letter to Frank Carlucci, then director of OEO, tells what happened after that:

"Dear Mr. Carlucci:

"I am very much disturbed by recent actions of the federal Office of Economic Opportunity in relation to the investigation of the California Rural Legal Assistance program and by the treatment being afforded the California State Office of Economic Opportunity by federal OEO.

"As you know, in January you made the determination that my veto of the CRLA grant should not be overridden. Subsequently, you requested that we agree to a full investigation of CRLA by a commission and to a new short-term grant for a period of six months. We agreed to your requests on the basis that this would be helpful in determining how best to provide legal services to the rural poor in the areas that have been served by CRLA.

"Since that time the federal OEO has repeatedly breached the understandings which had been agreed to by you and other federal representatives and by representatives of my office and the state OEO. Members of your office have made false and misleading statements to the news media with respect to the firm understanding which was reached jointly by the State of California and the federal government. Further, the selection process and the orientation of the commission were not conducted in accordance with our understandings. This has resulted in the commission members being confused and misinformed as to the nature and procedures of their task, and has severely hindered them in carrying out their responsibilities.

"If testimony presented before the commission during the past week is true, there has also been a lack of objectivity and fairness within federal OEO in reviewing my veto of CRLA and the reasons supporting it. This has even included threats to hold up the granting of federal funds for other projects totally unrelated to CRLA, unless California altered its position.

"The actions by the federal OEO, which are clearly detrimental to the best interests of the citizens of California, apparently have been taken in an effort to curry favor with the Poverty Laws Establishment, and to appease certain ultraliberal members of Congress who consistently oppose the President on every issue.

"The most recent misconduct is the premature release to the news media of a report criticizing the state OEO, in violation of an agreement that such a report would not be made public until after California officials had had the opportunity to respond with corrections of numerous factual mistatements and erroneous conclusions contained in that report. This premature release, and the resulting adverse publicity, seem calculated to create a smoke screen to mask the revelation of federal OEO's improprieties in regard to the commission investigating CRLA, and to aid those who are seeking to abolish any effective controls or safeguarding of OEO funds and programs within our state.

"It is interesting to observe that our state OEO has been 'reviewed,' 'evaluated,' and 'audited' by the federal government four times in the past four months—commencing immediately after the governor's veto of the CRLA grant. We are informed that this recent attention is greater than that shown any other state, a fact that raises at least a suspicion of bureaucratic harassment.

"At all times in our dealings with federal OEO, the State of California has acted in good faith, believing that the agreements to which we were a party would be honored by you and your subordinates. We have been repeatedly disappointed to find that this has not been the case.

"I am requesting that you take immediate action to rectify this situation, to insure that further understandings with our officials will be honored and to prevent further instances of misconduct of the type outlined above. By separate letter to the President, I am requesting that a meeting be set up which will include you, representatives of my office, and your superiors, to establish necessary safeguards to govern the relationships between the federal OEO and the State of California so that these types of incidents will not occur again. It is essential that corrective action be taken so that we can act together for the best interests of all the citizens of California, including those whom the Economic Opportunity Act was intended to benefit."

47

The governor's letter to President Nixon read:

"Dear Mr. President:

"Since our visit in January, John Mitchell and his staff have been of great assistance to us in attempting to resolve the problems with the federal Office of Economic Opportunity. I am very grateful to you for your personal interest and to John for his assistance.

"During the past few months, however, numerous problems have continued to arise from within the federal OEO, as some of their personnel appear unwilling to carry out the decisions and understandings reached between the State of California and the federal government. Enclosed is a copy of my letter to Frank Carlucci, which sets forth in detail these problems. Also enclosed is a copy of a letter that I was obliged to send to each member of the commission appointed to investigate the California Rural Legal Assistance program, to clarify our position and to advise them of the agreements made between federal OEO and my office.

"This situation has reached a point where the actions of federal OEO seriously jeopardize the ability of our state government to properly carry out its responsibilities under the Economic Opportunity Act and to assure our citizens that public funds are being properly used by OEO-funded agencies for the benefit of the poor. Therefore, I would appreciate your help in arranging a meeting which would include Frank Carlucci, representatives of my office, and such members of your staff as you may deem appropriate, so that we may resolve these problems and establish necessary safeguards to govern the relationships between federal OEO and the State of California. Such a meeting might be helpful to Mr. Carlucci because I am inclined to believe that sometimes members of his staff do not say to him the same things they say to us—or at least they shade it a bit. . . ."

One Washington proposal opposed by the Reagan administration was the Family Assistance Program of welfare reform advocated by the Nixon administration. Though the governor was never publicly critical of President Nixon, he felt that as a matter of principle he must oppose the Family Assistance Program. A letter to the President in 1970 sets forth the governor's misgivings:

"Dear Mr. President:

"My attempts to reach you on Monday and Tuesday having failed, I spoke with John Ehrlichman last evening. He felt

48

that Mr. Nathan, of the Bureau of the Budget, might help answer some of the serious questions, concerns, and reservations we have regarding the Welfare Reform Act, as it came out of the House, and is now being considered by the Senate.

"Mr. Nathan consulted with my staff at length. However, our general objections and reservations were outside his scope of authority. Additionally, while he expressed agreement with some of our objections, and even shared our concerns with one or two aspects, we received no assurance of what, if anything, the administration intends to do to amend the act accordingly.

"Meanwhile, I have today received a telegram from Chairman Long requesting my views on the proposed act. I intend to answer him fully and completely. I have been contacted by other governors and expect to have further conversations with them. In fairness to you and your administration, I hasten to send you herewith the essence of those reservations.

"In our meeting at San Clemente last August 13 when my staff and I had the opportunity to discuss welfare reform with you, we were elated at the proposals you outlined and, as I recall, offered to serve as a test state for the contemplated work-incentive part of the program you outlined.

"Since then, we have followed the progress of your program with a great deal of anticipation and, lately, apprehension. The evolution of the Welfare Reform Act—from your original message to the Congress on August 11, 1969, through Representative Byrnes' bill, to the Ways and Means Committee bill (HR 16311) as amended and passed by the House last week—has caused me increasing concern. Possibly you share that concern.

"My reservations about the Welfare Reform Act stem from a deep philosophical antipathy toward a government-guaranteed income and increasing federal intervention into state operations, and also my conviction that the bill will not accomplish your purposes as set forth in your August message to Congress. In addition, I have a real apprehension that the costs of the act will be excessive at a time when the taxpayer is already struggling to make ends meet.

"Let me set forth some of my specific concerns:

Work Incentive—
In your August message, you said, "I propose that we make available an addition to the incomes of the 'work-

ing poor' to encourage them to go on working and to eliminate the possibility of making more from welfare than from wages."

It seems to me that the act as passed by the House does *not* eliminate the possibility of making more from welfare than wages. It would be entirely possible for a family in which the father is fully employed to have less income than a family in which the father is working only part-time—and only slightly more income than if the father were not working at all. If you wish, we can supply specific data to support this statement.

Further, the act would encourage many now working their way off of the welfare rolls to fall back into a state of federal dependency.

Family Solidarity—

In your message to Congress, you said, "The new plan rejects a policy that undermines family life. It would end the substantial financial incentives to desertion." This is an objective which I support wholeheartedly.

But, under the Welfare Reform Bill as amended and passed by the House, very substantial incentives for desertion would remain. The bill could actually weaken incentives to maintain traditional family relationships and in some cases, may encourage dissolution of families.

Costs—

The act, as it came out of the House, appears to have all the earmarks of the open-ended welfare programs of the 60s—such as Medicare and Medicaid—whose costs have escalated beyond even the wildest sums predicted by their original opponents. Some of our staff predict— as do others in both the public and private sector—that the costs of this act could run as high as $15 billion.

I am convinced that, unless the Welfare Reform Act provides for funding solely from a specific surtax or dedicated tax, the taxpayers will be unaware of the extent of the real costs of the program and these costs will soon outpace any benefits which might be derived.

Government Income—

Although proponents of the new act claim it does not provide a government-guaranteed income, under this bill, no work-qualified head of household need actually

50

work. He, or she, is simply required to state a need and *agree* to work or train to work to receive benefits. This is—in fact—a guaranteed income. I must oppose such a proposal.

Federal Controls—

In order to advance your concept of "New Federalism," those states which are able and which desire to administer the program themselves should be paid rather than penalized for performing services for a federal program. Those states which are unable to administer their own programs, or do not desire to do so, should be charged—*not* rewarded—for having the federal government perform the services for them.

The disincentives in the act encourage states to surrender their administrative operations to Washington; this can hardly be compatible with your desire for a "New Federalism." The act delegates to the Department of Health, Education & Welfare, and Labor unprecedented administrative powers. This makes it impossible to assess how various provisions are to be applied, and what impact these will have on state operations now and in the future.

(It seems to me that one of the stultifying effects of the act will be to impede, in some cases destroy, the growing and creative work-program efforts being put forth by the private sector. This will stifle ingenuity and freeze failure; and, this is completely out of phase with emerging programs to solve these welfare problems at the local level. It is of deep concern that there are no provisions permitting the states to engage in, or continue, pilot projects which might prove more responsive to state or local needs.)

In order to support healthier relationships between the federal and state governments—and your efforts to limit the expansion of bureaucracy—the act should be amended to prohibit the formation of any new administrative organization except that which is necessary to audit and reimburse those states which administer their own programs, and to provide administrative services for those states which do not. This latter organization should be only as large as can be funded by the charges collected from those states which are serviced.

51

"In summary, Mr. President, your original proposal sought to reduce the welfare rolls; the bill passed by the House does not even mention this as a goal or purpose. It will add fifteen million persons to the system, with no significant reduction in sight, based on HEW estimates of continually rising costs.

"Your stated goal was to reduce welfare costs (also not mentioned in the new act); this program will cost additional billions, based on HEW estimates.

"Your message to Congress specifically rejected the concept of a guaranteed income; the new bill provides every family with an income floor.

"You called for manpower programs to get individuals off of welfare and on to payrolls; yet many, if not most, of the 'working poor' to be added to the rolls under the House-amended bill live in rural areas where there are no training facilities and where there are, in fact, no jobs to train for.

"I'm sure you know how painful it is to find myself in the position of opposing this measure. Only the strongest convictions could bring me to this, but after struggling with the ever-growing problems of welfare these past few years, I'm convinced this is the greatest single domestic problem facing the nation.

"It may be that working in concert we can remove the evils and correct the weaknesses of the House-passed bill and I offer my assistance."

Incidentally, although the President continued to support the proposed welfare program it did not pass the Congress. It is generally agreed that the governor's adamant and carefully reasoned opposition was the main reason for its eventual failure.

When Ronald Reagan first became governor, he and Mrs. Reagan were aghast at the mansion the state provided its governor. A wooden Victorian building, it had once been a boarding house. From its looks it might have housed the Adams family. But, because of its downtown location and the fact that it was a firetrap, it was not satisfactory for a governor with growing children.

Because of this the Reagans moved into a private residence in East Sacramento. When his landlord threatened to sell the house from under him, a group which included some friends of the Reagans joined together to buy the house and then rented it back to the governor.

This occasioned a humorous letter from the governor to "Dear Landlord," which went to each of the group.

"Knowing you receive unjustified complaints and undeserved criticism from miserable and unhappy tenants, and having a peculiar sympathy for anyone subject to that kind of treatment, I thought you might enjoy hearing from a happy tenant for a change.

"My wife and I are very glad you bought out our previous landlord. (He should lose the money on the way to the bank.) Somehow, the place looks brighter already, possibly because we painted a little here and there. (We won't knock out any walls, however, without letting you know.)

"Anyway, the hot water is hot when it should be; the neighbors are quiet. (If they complain, they'll get a freeway right through their piazza.) The fuses don't blow, even with all the lights on, and it's only ten minutes to my job.

"Just changing landlords has my wife so revved up she is pushing furniture all over the place (frankly, it gives me a pain in the back); but we want you to know we love you, we thank you, and if keeping the place real nice will help show our appreciation, we'll do it. We don't even let the dog in the house, and the kids are severely limited."

The governor penned a jesting P.S.: "I am talking to the people I work for about lowering your taxes."

Almost from the beginning, the governor hoped to persuade the legislature to approve construction of a mansion that would be adequate for future governors. But partisan bickering more than any one thing prevented construction getting under way until late in the governor's second term.

He and Nancy were destined never to live in a governor's mansion worthy of California, but future governors will, thanks to his efforts.

Letters to two legislators who opposed construction of the mansion on a river-bluff site about fifteen miles from the capitol tell of Governor Reagan's reasons for wanting it built.

To Robert Moretti, Democratic speaker of the Assembly, he wrote: "For almost forty years there seems to have been general agreement in Sacramento and elsewhere that California should have a new and suitable governor's residence. And yet for almost forty years such a project has foundered for the most part on the rocks of partisanship and bickering over

53

fairly unimportant differences. I would hate to see that happen again.

"Right now the issue of location has been raised and with it some misstatements as to how the present site was chosen. Being the only person at hand with personal experience in holding this job and living for a time in a downtown location, subsequently in a residential neighborhood, I'd like to offer some thoughts based on that experience.

"First of all, in this position it is difficult enough to maintain a normal family life and to raise children without making them live and grow up in a public edifice. I'm quite sure future governors are going to have school-age children. If the governor's residence is going to be downtown, a part of the capitol complex, who do they play with when they come home from school? I can attest to the fact that living in a downtown location they don't run out the back door and across the street or down the block to join schoolmates or neighborhood friends. This problem would be vastly multiplied if the original concept were followed of making the residence also house the executive offices. That's a great escape from the grist mill—taking an elevator from the office to an upstairs apartment. Believe me, a residence that is a home, and not an office complex, located in a residential neighborhood is a necessity."

In this letter Governor Reagan referred to the spurious contention that the proposed location was of archaeological value because it had been the site of either an Indian village or Indian burial ground or both. Some anti-Reagan Indians also used this issue as a reason to oppose the mansion. They were aided in that effort by the then secretary of state and present governor, Edmund G. Brown, Jr. Brown, a bachelor, on assuming office attempted in vain to stop construction of the mansion. For reasons unclear he has declared he will never live in it. Governor Reagan, however, believes future governors will.

In his letter to Moretti the governor discussed the Indian Village objection and ended with a plea for Moretti's cooperation:

"Since then the legislature has approved the site, appropriated the necessary funds, and an architectural firm has been selected in the manner prescribed by law. As for the possibility of the site being the locale of an ancient Indian village—this will only be known if an archaeological dig verifies it. If so, you have passed and I have signed a bill ordering that any remains be reinterred on the land in an area that will not be covered by structures. I would think that a plot could be set aside, properly marked and cared for. Incidentally, since archaeologists have declared that if such a village once existed there it was 3,000 years ago, I don't believe anyone alive today can claim relationship to those who lived in the village.

"Whatever our political differences, can't we go forward on this and at long last give California an official residence for its governors in a location that is as beautiful as anything the Sacramento area has to offer? This can be something of which all of us can be proud and for which future governors will be grateful."

In a letter to Assemblyman John Vasconcellos, also a Democrat, Reagan asked him to "reconsider your position," and pointed out that, "My predecessor, Governor Brown, and Mrs. Brown feel there should be a new residence and indeed were victims themselves of the political controversy that arose when they tried to bring this about. They've expressed their belief in the need after eight years experience in the job. Governors before them have been of like mind. Isn't there some significance to the fact that several governors of widely divergent views have been in agreement on this subject even when they no longer were personally affected?

"I think it would be a tragedy to relinquish the building site which has been given to the state, waste hundreds of thousands of dollars by halting construction and extend the forty years of political wrangling."

All of Governor Reagan's political letters were not to fellow office-holders or politicians. Neither did all of them deal with subjects as all-encompassing as tax or welfare reform or as personal as the mansion.

In one letter he opposed efforts to give California a unicameral (one-house) legislature. "There is much to be said for the check and balance and the added deliberative process in having two houses," he wrote. He believes that compromises worked out in conferences between two legislative houses are "good for the people in the long run."

In a letter to a "frustrated" constituent he explained a tax reduction and limitation program that eventually was to be submitted to the people in a special election. Known familiarly as "Prop. One," the proposal lost because, the governor was firmly convinced, people believed dishonest opposition

55

charges that it was really a tax-shift program. It was, perhaps, the only time the governor was unable to sell a program of his directly to the people of California. Here is his explanation of the proposal:

"When I say I share your frustration, let me point out the reason. No administration has worked harder at cutting the cost of individual programs and no administration has been more successful in reducing the cost of those programs. Yet, government continues to grow at every level in size and in cost. This is why we had a task force appointed over a year ago to see if there was some other way that government spending could be held down. They came in with this proposal for a fifteen-year plan of gradually reducing the percentage of your income the state could take without your permission, and then putting a limitation about 20 percent less than the present level at the end of that period, in the Constitution so that only by your vote—by a vote of the people—could government ever go beyond that limit. In addition, we added to this the rebate of 20 percent of this year's income tax and a proposal to reduce permanently the income tax by 7½ percent. Individuals with a taxable income of below $4,000 and families earning less than $8,000 will have no state tax-liability at all.

"I urge you to support this measure because it is probably the last chance to ever put a limitation on government spending. It can set the stage for a new approach in other states and even at the national level."

In the same letter he answered a number of other complaints from the frustrated constituent: "Now, as to your disillusionment with the party and the desired change, may I just remind you of a few facts, hopefully to set the record straight. What would the budget be if in addition to the Democratic majority in the legislature, there had been a Democratic governor with the same philosophy? I have vetoed out of the budget over these six years more than a billion dollars in increased spending that had been added in by the legislature after I sent the budget upstairs. The budget would be a billion dollars larger than it is had these vetoes not taken place. The only year since I have been governor that I did not have to veto any money out of the budget was the one year we had a Republican majority in the legislature. In that year the budget came down as I sent it upstairs, with no additional spending. In last year's budget alone I vetoed $503 million out. Now, in addition to this, I have vetoed appropriations and spending bills introduced throughout the regular legislative session. I have no total on those but it could well exceed another billion dollars. Last year I vetoed 168 measures. In every instance, the Democratic majority tried to override my veto but our Republican legislators held firm and our opponents could not get the two-thirds majority necessary.

"With regard to state-employee salary increases let me call your attention to what is mandated by law. The law says these employees must be paid comparable to salaries in the private sector for people doing comparable work. Three years ago we held our employees at no salary increase at all. Now, complying with the law and over a three-year period, we are making adjustments to bring them up to the level of the private sector.

"I agree with you that Watergate has had a very depressing effect upon our country. I don't think, however, it is fair to conclude that there are no dedicated people in government. Actually, the people in government are pretty much the same as in any group. They are no better or no worse than the people who send them there.

"If I may make one last point. You speak of politicians. I never in my entire life had any desire to run for public office. I was finally persuaded to do this by a group of people who shared my beliefs. I felt as you do that something had to be done. I gave up a career that was rewarding me at a rate of five times my present salary in government. I don't think of myself as a politician. I think of myself as a citizen who took this chore on to try and accomplish something."

Writing to the Rev. David R. Ellingson in 1974, Governor Reagan touched on the dangers of high costs of government. "I am convinced that this country must take the lead in controlling the cost of government which leads to inflation, and, thus stop this runaway increase in prices as well as the enormous tax burden being borne by the people. Until we do, we are going to see our standard of living for the great middle class of America continuing to decline. The worst part of all this is that not only does the standard of living decline, but we are saddling future generations with an unbearable debt because of our continued deficit funding."

Another problem that beset the Reagan administration in its early years was the very emotional issue of mental illness, and how much money the state should spend in caring for the mentally ill and the mentally retarded. This was another area in which reporters and people who were emotionally—or politically—involved ignored what the governor was attempting to do and attacked him as a man who put money ahead of humanitarian concepts and who was heartless and cruel.

In his continuing effort to keep the record straight, Governor Reagan as late as 1974 wrote to one father: "... I wanted to clear the air regarding some misunderstandings about our mental health-care policy and the possibility of hospital closings.

"In spite of what some hospital employees might say, there has been no economy move at the expense of the mentally ill. The program of transferring many patients from state hospitals to county mental health-care clinics is dictated by legislation passed several years before I became governor. Actually, our budget, staffing, and our per-patient cost has gone up considerably, and we do not regret this. The legislation I refer to was based on the professionals' belief that smaller, more localized treatment centers and hospitals could do a better job than the large state institutions which in too many instances had simply become warehouses providing only custodial care.

"The hospital population at the beginning of the bill was some 37,000. By the time I became governor it was 26,000. It has now been reduced to less than 10,000. In no instance, however, was anyone forced out of the hospital. They could only be removed when counties notified us they had the facilities and were now prepared to take over their citizens who were in the state hospitals. These county clinics, under the previous administration, were subsidized between 50 and 75 percent of the cost. We are subsidizing them at 90 percent of the cost. I will admit that we did find instances where counties were over optimistic, and in their desire to get operations underway, asked for patients when they actually did not have all the facilities required. We have taken, and are taking, steps to change this to make sure the counties can handle the cases properly.

"Naturally, as the hospital population declined, there were some closings and consolidations. Perhaps in the future there will be more. There is, however, no intention of totally eliminating the state hospital. We realize not only the need for

research but principally the need for custodia[l]
who cannot be helped by the smaller county [⋯]
done our best to make the employees in the s[⋯]
derstand the long-range plans and that there [⋯]
threat to these hospitals or to their positions. [⋯]
the rumor mill grinds and the morale persists. I have to say
that some of this, I feel, is engendered by employees who
have never believed in the legislation changing the policy and
are trying to retain the original concept of the large ware-
house-type hospital.

"In all of this, I know there are instances, and perhaps you
are the victim of one of these, where certain hospitals or even
certain wards within hospitals are not up to the standard
we have tried to maintain. Sometimes this is a temporary situation due to an inability to hire and fill positions. Sometimes
it's just slack administration."

The decline in numbers of mental-hospital patients early in
the Reagan administration brought a corresponding cut in
hospital staffing. Ignoring the fact that staff-to-patient ratios
remained *higher* than in any major state, opponents of the
governor accused him of cutting back on care for the mentally ill in order to save money. Despite all efforts to explain
the program to the public, some of the resentment against
Ronald Reagan, fostered by this false charge, lingered
throughout his entire eight years as governor.

The question of how elected public servants should be paid
was another that brought a letter from Governor Reagan to a
constituent: "I confess I don't have a totally satisfactory answer, but lean very much toward the idea of salary and al-
lowances, which make it possible for a dedicated individual
to serve even though he has no personal wealth. If we want a
man's best thinking applied to our community problems, we
should see that he is reasonably sure of being able to provide
for his family and the education of his children."

The governor also suggested that it would be of value to
have a study measuring whether "a George Meany rate[s] a
salary . . . nearly double that of a United States senator" or
whether a state university president should make more than
the governor of that state. It happens that in California the
president of the university system is paid more than the governor.

Another letter voicing a constituent's laundry list of complaints brought the reply that "I have been sitting here puz-

over how I can answer your letter without sounding like
politician making promises."

He then continued: "You spoke of unkept promises about
reform of welfare and some of the other things that are
wrong in government. May I just point out that many of us
who are supposedly making the promises are most sincere
and are trying to achieve the reforms. But we are frustrated
because vested interest groups, such as the Welfare Rights
Organization, the Welfare Workers Union, and numerous
groups created by OEO grants, have become powerful lobby-
ing forces able to launch widespread propaganda and able to
sway votes to keep reform efforts bottled up in legislative
committees or rejected in the final vote on the floor.

"I believe very deeply in the so-called 'silent majority,' the
people like yourself who make this country run, who send the
kids to school, pay the bills, pay the taxes, and only now and
then raise a voice as you have in legitimate protest. Further, I
have tried to keep myself in the position of representing that
'silent majority,' as obligated to stand between the taxpayers
and the tax-spenders. I am not alone in government. There
are many more who share that idea, but we very much need
the help of people like you. We need voices on our side when
we take stands against spending on behalf of the taxpayer because, heaven only knows, the capitol can fill up very fast
with the voices from those other groups.

"I have told this legislature we have reached a time for
choosing. We can meet our fiscal problems in government by
adding to your burden with more taxes, or we can have the
guts to cut back the size and cost of this government and reform welfare and stop giving money to people who are not
truly dependent on the rest of us. I choose this latter course.

"In these next few months you are going to see a very
bloody battle here in our capitol. I wish I could reply to your
letter with some assurance that automatically and immediately things are going to be better. I can only say, don't give
up just yet. You are not alone and there is going to be a
fight. And your help will be needed."

Agricultural problems also came to the governor's attention. In more than one case he had to disappoint his friends
in this great California industry. For instance, California's
peach growers, generally strong supporters of the governor,
wanted him to sign a bill that would have limited and con-
trolled the planting of cling-peach orchards.

Governor Reagan vetoed the bill and wrote to Ralph B. Bunje, general manager of the California Canning Peach Association, that "seldom has a bill caused me so much mental anguish as this one."

"I am well aware of the hardships and the problems affecting the peach growers, and as you know I have ordered Earl Coke and Jerry Fielder to bend every effort to see if they cannot find ways to help in this situation. I found, however, I could not in clear conscience sign the bill which arrived on my desk. It was contrary to everything I think is our philosophy, and not a valid answer to the present problem. Over the long run, the precedent it established would, in my opinion, be destructive of the very system we are trying to defend. It literally said that those now engaged in the business could, by their vote, keep anyone else from ever coming in. Growers from a half-dozen different crops were lined waiting with similar legislation. Believe me, I tried to find some reason within the bill which would permit me to sign it, and could not."

Turning down friends and then explaining "why" to them is one of the more uncomfortable duties a governor has. When old-time actor-singer Pinky Tomlin, a staunch Republican, called, recommending a friend for a judgeship, the governor replied by letter: "Confirming our recent phone conversations, I have to say with great regret that while your friend is qualified regarding a judicial appointment, there just seems to be in that particular area a great wealth of talent. Under the system we've been using of screening all possibilities through a variety of committees—local bar, local laymen, state bar and so forth—a number do come out ahead in the ratings.

"For all these four years, I've tried very hard to abide by this rating system so that those doing the ratings would realize not only did they have a responsibility, but that their careful screening was the basis upon which appointments were made. For that reason, I just can't skip down and make an appointment which would be obviously bypassing some of their choices.

"I know how much this means to you, and I'm sure your friend must be aware of all that you've done in his behalf. Let me just say we will of course keep his name here on tap in the event that any changes may occur. But again, I must say realistically, there are so many in this particular area that

I can't hold out too much hope. I know you'll understand. Again, my regrets."

No book about Governor Reagan would be complete without the mention of jelly beans. The governor and the jelly bean arrived in Sacramento simultaneously and they soon became a trademark of his office.

There were some misconceptions about them, as there always is when people begin trying to trace the growth of a tradition without going to the source.

This letter to Dr. Alcides Pinto, director of research at the Crownsville, Maryland, State Hospital, sets the record straight in the governor's own words.

"I'm afraid a certain amount of distortion has resulted from the distance the story traveled. Apparently a somewhat humorous incident has been portrayed as a system for breaking the smoking habit. Unfortunately, I have no such system.

"Some years ago when I gave up smoking I found the most trying times were those periods immediately after lunch and dinner—especially dinner. I began popping a few jelly beans in my mouth and that in itself became a habit.

"A friend delivered a large jar of jelly beans to me here in the capitol my first day in office. It was quite a joke for awhile, since I left the jar on the Cabinet Room table. Evidently no one really ever outgrows the childhood love for jelly beans. The jar has been refilled many times over these six years and our cabinet meetings go on with the jar being passed around during even the most solemn of meetings. Cabinet and staff have become jelly-bean users. There isn't a great deal of smoking in the meetings, but I don't know whether this can be credited to the candy.

"I'm sorry if the news stories have raised any false hopes."

In another letter, referring to "the place jelly beans have in this administration," the governor wrote, "some political figures have endured in history as lions or conquerers or something equally impressive. It's a little frightening to think California history might record us as jelly beans."

Rib ticklers usually drew responses from Governor Reagan who loves a funny story, a one-liner or a quip, although he groans at puns.

W. E. Bolton of Castro Valley wrote the following letter to the governor.

"Governor, I may never smile again!

"I am a man, you see, and I feel I have been cheated. I've

been listening to some women on television hold forth on this new fad called Women's Liberation and I developed a great feeling of emptiness in my chest. Women need to be liberated like a humming bird needs a flight manual.

"What I am saying isn't against women. Not in the least. I love women. They are good conversational companions; they bring light into a man's life.

"But I sneer at their current drive for liberation—whatever the hell that means.

"I know where women come from. God made the first one, Eve, from one of Adam's ribs . . . and I think that was where all the trouble started. It all boils down to simple jealousy!

"Women are jealous of men!

"But the peculiar thing is that men really should be jealous of women. Think about it. Who was the ugliest person you ever knew? Some man, right? And the prettiest? A woman, of course. Who gets all the proposals—not to mention the propositions. Women are first! Yes they are. What's the President's wife called? The First Lady. Did you ever hear of some famous woman's husband being saluted as the First Man? No. Only Adam has that honor.

"Some honor.

"Who let himself be carved up so Eve could be fabricated? Do you think for one minute she would have given up one of her bones to create man? A fingernail maybe, but God would have had a second hell on his hands if He'd asked a woman to part with anything substantial just to make a bedfellow.

"You know when I was just a boy growing up in the Bible Belt, it was an accepted fact that women have one more rib than does man.

"Of course they were wrong.

"There are two more in the female.

"Figure it out, she has all of hers, plus one of his; he has one less than all of his. Or, she has her full quota, plus one, while he has his full quota, minus one. Get it?

"Now what in hell is a poor rib-deprived man supposed to do?

"Governor, please give it some thought. Privately, I doubt that we will ever be able to get our rib back after all this time. But don't you agree that we ought to get something out of the deal?"

Governor Reagan responded:

"I have read your letter anent ribs and women with great interest.

"I am pleased to tell you I share your views about women's liberation. At the same time, I have to say I'm greatly pleased with the twenty-three ribs that have been assigned to me under the marital customs of our society. While I feel no need personally for the proposal you make to restore equity in the matter of the missing rib, I have asked my legal advisers to look into all the ramifications of such a change in the law.

"However, and above all, I want to thank you from the bottom of my heart for your letter. Your complaint about the missing rib is the only thing I haven't been blamed for since I've been in this damn job."

As the days of his administration dwindled the governor began receiving letters praising him for his outstanding record as governor. Because this is a book primarily of letters *from* the governor I must omit most of them, but nevertheless two or three, I think, are appropriate.

One, from Democratic assemblyman Wadie P. Deddeh, said in part: ". . . I have deemed it an honor and a privilege to work with you these past years.

"You have manifested a sincerity of purpose, an enormous amount of personal energy, a real dedication and a sense of philosophy which elevates political discussion to the high level of philosophy. . . .

"You and Mrs. Reagan, not unlike other good and past first families of our state, have consistently set for us an example of personal integrity and maturity of individual behavior that cannot be lost, as a lesson for our young people. . . .

". . . as you retire from the governorship, I would hope you will continue to be a voice of high philosophical character in the public dialogue of the coming years."

The governor, obviously touched, responded: "Your letter has to be one of the nicest things that's happened to me in these almost eight years. I thank you from the bottom of my heart."

Another unexpected letter came from a state-university administrator. "Well," began the letter, "I guess I need to say that, in my judgment and after eight years of your administration, you've been a damn good governor.

"There is of course the fiction that you've destroyed either the University of California or the California State University and Colleges, or both, but you know and I know—and every thoughtful, analytic person knows—that is not true. Indeed, in my judgment, while you might have been from time to time too tight on the reins your overall support for higher education, and especially the CSUC, has been adequate and beneficial.

"But your contribution has been in another direction, really: forcing us in higher education to reexamine our beliefs, our values, our directions, our policies, and procedures. In a certain sense your very early 'cut, squeeze, and trim' proposal (remember the 10 percent across-the-board cutback in early 1967?) got our attention in the same way the mule-master gets the attention of the mule—you sure got my attention, and in the last seven years I've come to see that a great deal, most if not all, of what you were trying to say to my colleagues and me surely makes sense, academically and fiscally.

"My 'conversion' started, but did not finish, during the year ... of greatest activism: the moratoria, the Cambodian incursion, and the actual use of violence. I think, until that year, I really didn't believe in my heart that faculty members could be so irresponsible, that their 'liberal principles' were so damn flexible as not to be principles but mere prejudices and whims. I learned; and you do not know it, but you helped teach me—you went to most [of] the CSUC board meetings then, and spoke, and I tried to listen and understand. Finally, I did.

"Hence this letter, which is an awkward attempt to express a kind of belated appreciation. You've been a good governor, and equally important, a good educator in the lessons you've taught. I only wish it were you, and not the governor-elect, who'd occupy your office for the next four years."

In his reply the governor said, "I'll take many memories and a very few mementos with me, and your letter will be one of those. You've made me very proud and truly grateful."

Finally, there is a last bit of correspondence between Ronald Reagan and S. I. Hayakawa. Hayakawa's letter is signed in Japanese, "Your favorite Samurai." Here are the letters:

"Dear Dutch:

"I want you to know, as you leave office, that it was a pleasure and an honor to have been a state college president during your administration. I want to thank you for the abundant moral and practical support you gave me, both before the general public and before the trustees of the state college system.

"Some of my academic colleagues foolishly regard you as an enemy of higher education because you insisted on professional responsibility in the faculty and civility among students.

"I want you to know that a majority of us, both professors and administrators, believe that you have been a good friend of education. Both the California State University and Colleges system and the University of California system have come a long way since the dreadful days of 1968, '69 and '70. You have helped enormously in bringing about this change.

"Every good wish to you in your future undertakings, whatever they may be.

"Sincerely yours,

"(Translation: Your favorite Samurai.)"

"Dear Samurai:

"Your letter is more appreciated than words can tell and it shall be kept with those very special things I take with me when I leave. Indeed, it is my only letter from a campus president in either of the two systems.

"It seems a long way back to those dark days when you breeched the barricade. Yet in some ways it seems only yesterday. I believe it marked a turning point in the insanity that gripped so much of academia and you were very much responsible for the turning.

"Again, I thank you and I hope our paths will cross often in the days ahead."

The Citizen-Politician

I consider myself very fortunate. In a time when many Americans have become cynics about their government and their elected representatives, I feel confident and ever more devoted to our system. Why? Because I have had an opportunity to observe firsthand how it works and who makes it run.

Granted, not all aspects of politics are appealing. Campaigns and an all-encompassing desire to win on the part of those participants can bring out the worst in people. And there are those public servants who take advantage of their positions, don't do their homework, and base their actions solely on the votes they may bring.

I do not say it is wrong for officeholders to listen to the people. It is essential that those in government do listen. However, there is a greater duty. If, as an elected official, you gain information which suggests that many people are wrong or misguided in their support of or opposition to an issue, you have a responsibility to inform them and to act in their best interest, as you see it, regardless of the consequences. It's always disheartening to see a greater number of legislators than I would like to admit take the easy way, instead of the principled way, in order to assure their re-election. But then there are statesmen, like Ronald Reagan, who are as forthright champions of the people and their own principles as you could ever find.

I know that the answer to the problems of our state and nation is to find and elect better candidates, not to change the system which has served us well for nearly 200 years.

Being a politician doesn't always make one an object of unqualified admiration. Ronald Reagan knew this before he ever sought office. Hence his description of himself while running for governor the first time, as a "citizen-politician." But to some people a politician is a politician is a politician. And that viewpoint brought a reply to a letter from Mrs. Marjorie P. Gallion of Crane, Texas.

"I take exception," the governor wrote, "to one line in your October 20 letter. That is that I am a politician and therefore undeserving of your unqualified support."

Then he explained: "... I came to this job never having sought it, never having believed that I should be in public office, and believing only that a set of circumstances had placed me here as a citizen with an opportunity to do something in behalf of the philosophy and the ideas which I supported. I have repeatedly told my cabinet and staff that we belong here only so long as we refer to government as 'they,' and never think of government as 'we.' I made a pledge to myself that I would make every decision on the basis that I would never run for office again. I didn't mean that I wouldn't run, but I felt that the first time a man in public office makes a decision on the basis of what it might or might not do with regard to votes in the next election, he has begun the path of compromise from which there is no turning back. I have kept that pledge."

The letter, written in 1971, was one of a number of pre-Watergate letters in which he strongly defended President Nixon. He wrote: "All I tried to indicate to you in my last letter was that the President had to deal with things as they are, not as he would like them to be. Bluntly, he inherited a situation in which the Democratic leadership had allowed the strength of this nation to deteriorate until we are in a situation where the possibility exists of the Soviet Union delivering an ultimatum. Since the President is the only man with access to all the information and all the facts necessary for a decision, I believe we must permit him to make those decisions, making sure, of course, that he is aware of the basic feelings of our people. It is my opinion that President Nixon has not shown that he goes along with the appeasement policy of the previous administrations. If I am wrong in this, I will be the first to repudiate him. Until such time, however, I believe we should go along with his decisions."

Time and again the governor explained in letters that "I gave up a career I loved—certainly an affluence I could never hope to match in public life—all at the very point when I could have both my career and the leisure to enjoy the hobby and sport (ranching) which I loved as much as my career."

"Does it seem rational," he asked in one letter, "that I would make such a sacrifice and then for political expediency go against those convictions?

"When my present term is up, I've made it plain I'll not seek another. I've also made it plain I want no federal appointment. I intend to serve as governor, God willing, through these next three years.

"My beliefs now are the beliefs I held when I first ran for this office, when I campaigned for Barry Goldwater in '64, and for the years previous to that when, as a citizen, I traveled coast to coast speaking on behalf of conservative principles. Indeed, I chose to continue speaking even when to continue meant the loss of my television show."

Here, again, he was writing to a person obviously disillusioned with President Nixon prior to Watergate. "Yes," he admitted, "there are things I might have chosen to do differently [from Nixon] but ... I believe there is a better chance to advance my conservative principles with a Republican president, even though I disagree with some of what he does. I believe we have a better chance to elect a conservative president in 1976 if he doesn't have to run against an incumbent Democrat. I believe this country could very well cease to exist as a free nation if [a certain] one of the present Democrat challengers should be in charge for these next four years."

Governor Reagan always looked on Richard Nixon not only as the President but also as a fellow Republican, as a person of generally conservative political philosophy, and as a friend.

As one American who greatly respects the office of the presidency, the governor has been loath to attack any President, whether it was Truman, Eisenhower, Kennedy, Johnson, or Nixon. He has tried to keep his criticisms impersonal and aimed at the issues, not at the person.

Because he campaigned strenuously for President Nixon's election—and re-election—the governor felt a special obligation to give the President as much support as possible as he attempted to solve our country's most pressing problems and, at the same time, put it on a more conservative course.

As a friend the governor was always prepared to walk the extra mile with President Nixon, which he did in the case of Watergate, over the protests, I might add, of many of his political advisers. Many of these advisers felt that President

Nixon had not returned the kind of friendship and loyalty given him by the governor. Many felt, also that because of his strong defense of Nixon up until the day Nixon admitted his early knowledge of the Watergate cover-up, the stigma of the scandal would rub off on the governor and hurt his political career.

People who have the governor's best interests at heart sometimes forget that he always does what he thinks is the right thing and the decent thing—remember, in an earlier chapter where he talks about "always do and say the kindest thing"—regardless of how much others think it might hurt him.

I think one of the reasons Governor Reagan remained popular with the people of California all during his eight years in office is that he never forgot this and they instinctively always knew it of him.

But though he has "done and said the kindest things" about the former president it is plain to those who know him that Governor Reagan was deeply hurt and disappointed not only by Nixon's resignation but also by the actions and statements that finally came to light and forced his resignation.

The few instances of wrongdoing or the appearance of wrongdoing in his own administration were dealt with swiftly and firmly by the governor. As a result, his was one of the most scandal-free administrations in California's history. It is difficult for him to understand why President Nixon was unable to do likewise.

In still another letter the governor protested that "I didn't want to be a candidate or an officeholder. I didn't seek it, indeed I fought against it and then gave up a pattern of living I had worked a long time for." But he went on to say that "I am not complaining—this has been the most soul-satisfying thing I've ever done, but only because I, too, believed in a principle and am realizing the joy of battling, yes, and sacrificing to implement that principle."

Here, too, he contrasted his continuing support of Nixon's philosophy and actions to those of the Democrats. "I do not believe he has departed from his basic Republican philosophy. Certainly there is deficit spending and controls, but there is also a near runaway inflation he inherited, plus the economic dislocation that comes from winding down a war. I happen to know that he considers the measures he felt he had to take as bitter medicine for a temporary illness. By contrast, our Democratic opponents would control the economy on a permanent basis and have expressed a belief in an ongoing program of deficit spending in good times as well as bad.

"Perhaps the China visit is viewed with alarm. But what do we know of the intricacies of a worldwide chess game in which we are no longer number one militarily? The eight years of Camelot and the Great Society wasted away our defenses to an extent far more dangerous than most of us appreciate. Isn't it possible that the President is playing for time and elbowroom, aware that two potential enemies are presently at odds with each other? Aren't we better off if Russia feels it has to keep those 140 divisions on the Chinese border?"

In 1971 and early 1972 conservative protests about President Nixon often took the form of asking the governor to run against him. He always refused. Here is a letter to Ron Docksai, national chairman of the Young Americans for Freedom, that is typical of those refusals:

"Dear Mr. Docksai:

"I have just learned (from the press) of the plans Y.A.F. has for carrying on a presidential campaign in my behalf. While I am naturally proud that you hold me in such high regard, I still must ask with all the urgency I can express that you desist. To publicly repudiate any activity of Y.A.F. is not something I'm eager to do but, in this instance, I'll have no alternative if this effort continues.

"Let me presume on some seniority in the cause which has united us and plead with you to reconsider your position on Vietnam. It has been my privilege as a governor to receive in-depth briefings on the war and the international situation. As a result, I'm in full support of the President's Vietnamization policy.

"It is impossible to view Vietnam without taking into consideration where it fits into the gigantic chess game called the cold war. The stakes in that game are no less than our very existence and only the President has access to all the facts necessary for each move.

"We've come a long way since those pre-Goldwater days when there were so very few of us sounding the alarm. We've elected a President, but he is opposed by a hostile Congress determined to deny almost every request he makes. The great permanent structure of government, the bureaucracy, resorts to outright sabotage as part of the effort to put back in power those who will renew the 'trip' this country was on for the eight New Frontier and Great Society years.

"The move you've announced can only divide and destroy our chance to go forward. I am pledged to support the President and have told him I'll lead a California delegation to the convention in his behalf. I ask you to join me in this lest we awaken to find those who oppose our dreams and goals returned to power. Ours is an uphill and long-term fight against a combination of mass media and political forces who deny everything in which we believe. We cannot afford division."

The governor, as a Republican, publically supported President Nixon whenever possible, and when he differed with him on an issue, as he freely but privately admitted he sometimes did, he refused to take his differences to the press. But that kind of loyalty, though it held conservatives in line and helped the President over many rough spots, was not, in my opinion, reciprocated by the President. Neither was it enough for some old-line Nixon supporters.

Many of these had never forgiven Reagan for making a run for the presidency in 1968 nor had some of them forgiven him for winning the 1966 California Republican gubernatorial primary. They had wanted one of their own, former San Francisco Mayor George Christopher, to be governor. The people of California, however, made the final decision.

Some political decisions, or rather decisions made about politics, can cause bitterness and unhappiness in old friends and political allies. One such case arose when the governor broke his own rule by supporting a candidate in a Republican primary. Another of the GOP candidates was, like the first, a Reagan friend and supporter. He wrote to him that "I'm sure you can tell from what I've been saying lately, I am deeply, deeply disappointed and hurt by the position of those who claim to lead my party and its office holders—often, like yourself, my friends as well—who have given their endorsement to [the other candidate] in his campaign against me."

The governor responded:

"I have received your letter and am terribly sorry about the situation in which we find ourselves. I have always been aware of your great service and loyalty to the party and have admired and respected you for it. I didn't know you were even considering this race, but let me explain my obligation

72

to Newt, and I hope this will do something to indicate to your wife that I do try to return favors even if, in this instance, you seem to be the victim.

"Several years ago when we had just obtained a bare majority in the legislature and it looked as if we were, perhaps, going to be able to build on that and finally get out from under the years we've had here of bucking a Democratic majority, Newt had a great opportunity, but it would have eliminated our one-point lead in the assembly. I'm speaking of the vacancy created in his congressional district. Newt was beseeched by all his friends to seek that office, and I don't think there is any question but that his election would have been automatic. He would today be a United States congressman. I asked him, on behalf of the party, to stay in the assembly and help us maintain the bare majority we had achieved. He did a lot of soul-searching and then came in one day and said out of loyalty to the party he would stay here and forego the opportunity for congress. I told him then he had an IOU that not only myself but the party owed him and owed him well. He never called on me for any kind of favor until John Harmer's appointment and then he said to me that now, once again, he wanted to make a run for something other than the assembly and this was it, John's senate seat.

"I didn't see how I could do anything but support him in view of the generous thing he had done several years ago and the promise I had made. You know how I have observed neutrality during all these years, but now I come down to my last two months in office, my last chance to repay a debt, an obligation which I made several years before and I feel I had no choice. As I said before, I had no way of anticipating that you might be interested in this race and for that I am sorry. I repeat you have been a loyal ally and I owe you a great debt of gratitude. I hope you can understand, however, that in this instance, I had a commitment I could not ignore."

Many of the governor's letters attempt to interpret the President's pre-Watergate actions to others. In a letter to an old friend, Ben T. Shaw, publisher of the *Dixon Evening Telegraph*, he wrote:

"I think the President has a consuming desire to resolve the international situation and, frankly, has little concern or interest in domestic problems. For this reason, I think he entrusted the domestic problems to people not in keeping with his philosophy. I know he has been misinformed as to some legislative proposals, such as supporting the welfare bill. Senator John Williams heard the briefing given to him by HEW and told a fellow senator that if he did not know what he knows about welfare he would have favored the bill on the basis of that briefing.

"I suppose that what I'm saying is that the President is still of a basic philosophy that has not changed. But he needs to involve himself more in the great domestic problems. Here, I believe, we can have an effect. I don't think we've done enough to call these matters to his attention, or to influence him in another direction. I also believe that he is becoming more aware of the need for more involvement in domestic affairs.

"Knowing the defense posture he inherited, plus the peace sentiment sweeping the country and the shaky financial situation, I believe he has done well on the foreign scene. He told me the other day directly in answer to my question that if Red China attempts to take back Taiwan by force this country will protect and defend Taiwan. He told me also with regard to the Amchitka blast that even if the supreme court had ruled that he should not trigger the blast, he was going to go ahead and do it anyway regardless of the consequences, because it was so vital to our national defense.

"With this in mind and with the possibility of a Democratic victory, which we absolutely cannot afford, I have to say that I believe we should go forward in insuring his re-election, but at the same time not be hesitant about exerting pressure to secure passage of more conservative policies. I think his recent veto of the Child-Care Bill which I had talked to him about is an indication of what I said a few lines back about his growing awareness of the importance of his domestic decisions. There certainly is nothing wrong with you pressuring him editorial-wise toward more conservative decisions, but my hope would be that you would do this as a supporter urging a course of action rather than giving the impression of one who has chosen a different course."

In a letter to M. Stanton Evans, head of the American Conservative Union, the governor discussed Nixon's visit to Red China, a visit that upset many conservatives.

"Stan, let me suggest something about the China visit that, unfortunately, the President can't say, or for that matter, I can't say publicly without blowing the whole diplomatic game plan. It is true the President dressed this visit up in all the proper diplomatic, peaceful-coexistence, forgive-and-forget trappings that are so much a part of the great international chess game. It is also true that this does confuse and disturb Republicans who have believed in his hardheaded knowledge of the communists, if in nothing else. But let's look at it as a move in a very dangerous game where the stakes are freedom itself. You and I know that a President of the United States can really and practically no longer pursue the policy of peripheral containment of communism. American public opinion will no longer tolerate wars of the Vietnam type, because they no longer feel a threat, thanks to the liberal press, from communism, and they cannot interpret those wars as being really in the defense of freedom and our own country.

"Russia is still enemy number one. Russia is the country that very shortly will have the power to deliver an ultimatum. So the president, knowing of the disaffection between China and Russia, visits China, butters up the warlords, and lets them be, because they have nothing to fear from us. Russia, therefore, has to keep its 140 divisions on the Chinese border; hostility between the two is increased; and we buy a little time and elbowroom in a plain, simple strategic move, a million miles removed from the soft appeasement of previous Democratic administrations."

Reagan's support of the American presence in South Vietnam brought unhappy letters from some. One, from a young naval ensign, brought these thoughts in reply: "I can't help but think that the things you see today and which are disturbing to you, and certainly to all of us, are not the result of America being where it shouldn't be, but possibly the result of America forsaking its principles several years ago by asking men to fight and die for a cause that by some strange reasoning we said, at the same time, was not a cause worth winning."

He pointed out that "War very often brings out the noblest in men. By the same token, particularly when it drags on the way this has with no apparent goal in sight, it can bring out the worst. I fear very much this has happened. All I would suggest is, not that you lose your repugnance for the evils you see around you, but that you not let that distort your thinking with regard to the rightness or wrongness of America's position in the war against totalitarian aggression. Very simply, that is what this conflict is all about. It is not America who

75

has said we seek to impose our will on the world. It is the Communist combine subscribing to the ideology of Karl Marx, which has said we will not be satisfied until we have imposed our way on the entire world."

In his letters the governor did not hesitate to contrast the Republicans to the Democrats. In one to Thomas B. Meek of Santa Barbara he wrote: "All the potential Democratic candidates for President are saying the same thing in almost identical terms: 'Turn the country around—change direction.' Do they really mean that? Or do they mean, stop the change in direction and return to the eight years of Camelot and the Great Society, when we talked of long hot summers and accepted burning cities and rioting campuses as a matter of course, a way of life? They mired us down in a land war in Asia, doubled the budget, and ran the national debt up by seventy billion dollars—more than the combined debt of all the nations of the world. Inflation doubled and quadrupled, and we didn't let ourselves think how close we were to carrying our money in a basket. They declared war on poverty and couldn't win that one either.

"Somehow, a myth has gained wide acceptance that our opponents are the party of good times and prosperity. Many of our sons and daughters have been spoon-fed this myth in too many social science courses. These young people complain of regimentation by an impersonal bureaucratic government, of unsolved problems of human misery, and of war. And then, with a distorted perspective of history, we are told they are registering two to one in the party that presided over all these things. It is time to expose the myth; time to tell our sons and daughters we, too, are against these things; time to let them know we weren't running the shop when all this came into being.

"A Republican President has occupied the White House only eleven of the last forty years, and in only one two-year term did a Republican President have a Republican congress. This was the only two-year period in which the dollar did not depreciate in value. We have known four wars in my lifetime, all under Democratic administrations. And in the last forty years the only time we have known full employment, it has been the result of one of these wars. After six years of the New Deal, twenty-five percent of our workers were unemployed. World War II brought full employment. The next time, it was the war in Korea. A Republican President ended that one, and for eight years no young American was asked to die for his country.

"Now another Republican president is ending another war. In the transition to a peacetime economy there is a certain dislocation. Two million former servicemen and defense workers have joined the labor pool, and so we have temporary unemployment. Three hundred young Americans are not dying each and every week in a far away jungle. It would seem that unemployment, like wine, has vintage years. Today it is a crisis. We are told we are in a recession and, yet, unemployment is no higher today than it was during all those three years of Camelot. But then unemployment was taken for granted. In two years of frequent press conferences, President Kennedy was never asked once if he intended doing anything about unemployment. Only when they revved up to a full-scale war in Vietnam did we have full employment.

"The Democratic myth is built on false claims and a denial of reality. For thirty-eight of the last forty years, this nation's policy has largely been determined by a Democratic leadership which long ago abandoned the principles of Jefferson and Jackson.

"Today millions of Democrats and our own sons and daughters seek a course to believe in. There is a hunger today for spiritual values. Our people yearn to believe in their country and in themselves. Let that be our cause."

In a letter to a corporate executive he explained why he had become opposed to allowing corporations to contribute to campaigns: "I have become alarmed at a fairly recent development in the political process, namely the support—usually unreported by organized labor and government-employee organizations. In 1968 C.O.P.E. spent $68 million on the Humphrey campaign and only about $15 million had to be reported as contribution. The ruling group of our state employee's association this year announced they were going to contribute $500,000 to the candidate for governor who would 'do the most for them.'

"Yet in the 'Watergate' hysteria we see 'business' attacked as the source of all evil and curbs suggested on corporations but not on union practices. I don't believe there is any way to curb labor except by a blanket rule. Furthermore, labor's contributions do not reflect the actual preferences of the rank and file. Indeed many union members are compelled to support candidates who are not their choice. There is no way that even the biggest corporate givers can match this abuse of the democratic process by labor.

"I hope corporations and unions will urge their people—employees, stockholders, customers, and members to vote and contribute, and even which way to vote and contribute, but let's halt a handful of labor bosses from acting as power brokers in the name of millions of constituents who aren't even consulted as to their wishes.

"Incidentally, I will oppose to the end public funding of campaigns. We are agreed on the danger inherent in that."

Not all of the governor's unfriendly letters were from political enemies, as we have seen. By the same token some of his political enemies wrote friendly letters.

Bob Moretti, then speaker of the assembly, reacted to a personal attack on the governor, with a handwritten letter that began, "This is a very harsh business sometimes. There are occasions, however, when people go too damn far in attempting to make the other fellow look bad; I don't like it when it happens to me and I'm sure you feel the same.

". . . when a government official is attacked without reason it's unfair to him, his family, and all who are taken in by it. I'm sorry this happened."

The governor responded, "Just a quick line to tell you how very much I appreciate the note you had delivered to me over the weekend. You were kind to write as you did, and I'm most grateful.

"Sometimes I get concerned, not just with attacks on ourselves as individuals, but what we may be doing to the very structure of government. It seems lately there has been a growing disrespect, not for the officeholder so much as for the office itself, whether that be in the legislative or in the executive branch. This could pose a great danger to everything that I think we both want."

Another personal attack on the governor brought a strange and touching exchange of correspondence between him and Representative Jerome Waldie, a California Democrat.

Waldie had attacked the governor for his unfortunate remark—yes, even Ronald Reagan slips once in a while—that "It's just too bad we can't have an epidemic of botulism" in the food distribution program brought about by the Patty Hearst kidnapping.

The governor explained publicly that the statement "was

made at a completely private gathering. I used a very ludicrous statement to simply express the frustration."

Waldie, however, who was in the midst of a losing campaign for the Democratic nomination for governor, refused to accept the explanation. In a public statement of his own, Waldie said that "insensitive, heavy-handed ugly attempts at humor on the part of the governor ... must only add to the dangers Patty Hearst is already experiencing. I don't expect the governor to understand the problems and the tragedy of poor and hungry people, but surely he must recognize that his irresponsible comments endanger Patty Hearst. Governor, keep quiet, please."

That remark brought this letter from the governor:

"Dear Jerry:

"Ordinarily, I wouldn't write a letter like this in reply to a public statement, and if you've been misquoted in the attached article, ignore this one. In case the article is accurate, however, I'm writing because of late I've become increasingly concerned about the harshness with which all of us seem to react with regard to our differences.

"I realize that you and I approach our jobs from a different philosophical viewpoint and, yet, in times past men of good will could disagree, debate their differences, and do so without the animus that characterizes today's political rhetoric.

"You assail me for 'insensitivity and endangering Patty Hearst' and yet I have scrupulously refrained from public comment and have explained to the press at every opportunity my reasons for not answering their questions. The remark of mine you are quoted as saying was 'ugly, heavy-handed humor' was, as the news story indicates, uttered in a private gathering and certainly not as a joke. I find nothing to joke about in this terrible and tragic situation.

"It was one of those exaggerations we all at times utter to express frustration and we do so with the confidence that no one takes us literally. How often do we say 'I'd like to tear him limb from limb' or 'I'd give a million dollars,' etc.?

"Some individual, however, for his own purposes, felt compelled to phone a single reporter who then proceeded to publicize my unfortunate choice of words. I can only assume that he placed a greater importance on embarrassing me than on protecting a kidnap victim.

TRIAL OFFER

You can subscribe to the RIGHT REPORT and receive 10 issues for just $12. Or, if you wish, you can start a full year's subscription for just $24. And you can deduct $2 from the price of either offer, if your payment accompanies your order. If you are not completely satisfied, you can cancel and we'll refund the unused portion of your subscription.

To subscribe to THE RIGHT REPORT, send to:

THE RIGHT REPORT
7777 Leesburg Pike
Falls Church, Virginia 22043

"You then (if you are correctly quoted) go on to say that you don't expect me to understand the problems and the tragedy of the poor and hungry people. This is an example of the political rhetoric I mentioned. Jerry, I assume we all want to help the less fortunate as well as all our citizens—that's why we are in public life—or at least it should be our reason.

"I don't know too much about your background and obviously you don't know about mine except for the widely publicized occupation I once was in. But let me assure you I do understand the 'problems and the tragedy of poor and hungry people.' I grew up as one of them. Knowing poverty at first hand has left me deeply imbued with a belief that opening opportunities for the poor to improve their lot is the only acceptable solution to this greatest of all human miseries.

"Handouts at the price of a young girl's life are not an answer—we'd soon run out of young girls. Obviously, we must provide for all who need help, but we should do so always with the conviction we are doing this as a stopgap until we can make them self-sustaining. Seven years ago, California's labor department was ineffectual—unwanted by job hunters or those who offered employment. Last year we found jobs for 275,000 Californians; 59,000 of them were welfare recipients. In the last six months of this fiscal year we have already moved 37,000 welfare people into private-industry jobs.

"The two-party system should be like our variety of churches—we are all headed in the same direction, we just have different ways of getting there."

And this response from Waldie:

"Dear Governor:

"You are quite right in your gentle admonition to me concerning the excessive rhetoric I used in responding to your reported off-the-record remarks about botulism.

"I know you are not insensitive and I know you care. I also believe your personal childhood experiences must have made the impact on your views of the necessity of assisting the poor that you describe.

"I am sorry, Governor. We can all do better in this process and you were correct in noting my deficiencies in this regard.

"Your letter was a touching and a moving one. We should all develop the grace in responding to an injustice that you exhibited in that letter.

"I don't know if you desire to release my apology publicly,

but be assured that I would have absolutely no objections in your doing so.

"Thank you, Governor, for helping me toward understanding."

The Spirit of the Man

Ronald Reagan is a sensitive man, perceptive, and with an instinctive kindness in his make-up. He is also unashamedly moral and deeply religious. He has a strong belief that the Lord's will plays a part in the affairs of men and that faith in the Lord is essential if a man is to achieve great things.

It is this faith that sometimes approaches fatalism that not only is one of the governor's greatest strengths but also is a trait that frustrates some of his associates who from time to time worry that nice guys don't always finish first.

The following letters and excerpts say something about the governor's religious beliefs, personal philosophy, and approach to life.

In a letter to Vera Gailey of Rialto, California, he wrote, "You asked for a prescription for living and that's a big order indeed. You know, man in his entire history has adopted about four billion laws—and we haven't improved the Ten Commandments an iota.

"Perhaps you illustrated a good prescription with your kind letter. About as simple a rule as I know is—'always do and say the kindest thing.' "

He spoke of his faith in a letter to Mr. and Mrs. L. W. Ripple of Bakersfield, California. After thanking them for "telling me about the people of your church and your prayers for me," he added, "I believe very much in His promise that, 'where two or more gather in My name, there will I be also.' I think I have known and felt the power and help of those prayers."

In a letter to Billy Graham he wrote that, "Like you, I walk between that pessimism expressed by your congressman and newspaper friends and my own optimism based on faith."

Continuing, he turned to a discussion of some of today's religious trends. "For a long time now I have been opposed to the young people's rejection of the church; at the same time they seem to be turning to Christ. Now I wonder if they haven't sensed something in advance of the rest of us. It fills me with terror to think of seminaries turning out class after class of clergymen who, apparently, are more social worker than minister, and to read of an entire denomination teaching young people to approach the Bible with their own beliefs as to what they should and should not accept."

Then he added, "It has always seemed to me that Christ in His own words gave us reason to accept literally the miracle of His birth and resurrection. He said, 'I am the Son of God.' Indeed, He said so many things that we have a very simple choice: either we believe Him, or we must assume He was the greatest liar who ever lived. If we believe the latter, then we have to ask, could such a charlatan have had the impact on the world for two thousand years that this man has had? We have known other great fakers down through the centuries. Some are even a paragraph in history. None had a lasting effect.

"I don't think I am one who believes the church should completely abandon its concern for man's physical being, but heaven help us if the church's concern in this direction makes it forget its responsibility for our spiritual welfare. Jesus was very explicit, it seems to me, about man finding salvation in his own soul, making the determination that he personally would do good. Somehow, it seems, the church is copping out if it substitutes for conversion the coercion of government and the taxing power to make people do good through government programs, whether or not they have made the decision in their own hearts that they want to do good."

In response to a letter from a woman protesting the teaching of evolution in the public schools the governor pointed out that "I can't impose a dictate on the board," but then went on to say, "Somehow I've never had any trouble reconciling spiritual and scientific versions of creation. God's miracles are to be found in nature itself; the wind and waves, the wood that becomes a tree—all of these are explained biologically, but behind them is the hand of God. And I believe this is true of creation itself."

To another constituent he wrote: "I could not bear this job for a day if I did not have an abiding faith in God and if I did not feel I could call upon Him for help. I do believe we are bound to help our less fortunate brothers. I believe also that Christ made it plain this should come from our hearts

83

voluntarily. Indeed He resisted those who suggested that, as a king, He should order compliance."

In a letter to the Reverend John J. McVernon, of the Narcotic Addiction Control Commission at the Brooklyn, N.Y., Central Rehabilitation Center, he discussed a meeting he had had with Pope Paul. The Pope, he said, "has been most helpful to the United States in the international effort to reduce the drug traffic."

He continued, "However, he [the Pope] was concerned about whether this alone could solve the problem. I told him of my own feeling that it could not, that it was almost like carrying water in a sieve, and that only a program that would make our young people voluntarily reject drugs could eventually do the job. I told him of the so-called 'Jesus movement' in America and how so many young people had simply turned from drugs to a faith in Jesus. As you can imagine, he was not surprised, nor should we be, for He promised that He was our salvation."

His reliance on religion came through, too, in a reply to a letter protesting present-day sexual permissiveness.

"I don't believe the answer rests with government," he wrote, "No one can legislate morality. What we need is a spiritual awakening and return to the morals of a Christian society."

In another letter in response to a question, he touched on the same subject: ". . . no, I am not supporting the movement to abolish or lessen the present laws concerning sexual conduct. I am deeply concerned with the wave of hedonism—the humanist philosophy so prevalent today—and believe this nation must have a spiritual rebirth, a rededication to the moral precepts which guided us for so much of our past, and we must have such a rebirth very soon."

But the governor was able to joke a little about the subject, also. A constituent sent him a clipping in which a state senator who favored prescribing birth control devices for teen-age girls without parental consent charged that "illegitimate births to teen-aged mothers have increased alarmingly while Reagan has been in office."

Reagan replied: "Thanks very much for sending me the clipping . . . I have never felt quite so young and virile." He added on a serious note that "I can't rid myself of the idea that someone should perhaps be reasoning with teen-age girls before they get pregnant, rather than throwing up our hands and trying to figure out how to eliminate the consequences of their acts."

Most people who know him agree that during his eight years as governor Ronald Reagan changed very little. Asked to write his observations on changes which occur in an individual who becomes famous, the governor responded: "I believe that a mature person will not change very much at all. This person will express the traits and attitudes in the new setting which were true before. Some individuals who become subject to considerable public attention before they have 'grown up' are less predictable. Though the same person is there as before, becoming used to a loss of privacy or to attention—deserved or sometimes less deserved—may bring about unexpected aggressiveness or shyness, unnoticed conceit or humility. I would suggest that the main question has to do with the personality, not with fame."

He penned a P.S. to the letter: "In my previous career—motion pictures—we had a truism about people who 'went Hollywood'—they always were that way. Hollywood just exposed it."

The spirit of Christian forgiveness shone through in a letter to a youth who had threatened to bomb the state capitol. The boy wrote to apologize for what he called "a prank." The governor wrote back: "I appreciate and accept your apology and do forgive you. I think I understand also something of what caused you to do what you did. You say you have learned your lesson and will never play another prank of this kind again. I hope that this is really true and that you have learned the hurt that can come from what seems to be a harmless joke.

"As the years have gone on, I have come to the conclusion that the so-called practical joke can rarely be played without someone actually being hurt, sometimes very seriously. I won't go into detail about what happens in a capitol such as ours when a threat is received but will only say in these days of terrorist activity when so many real threats and real bombings occur, the possibility of tragedy arising from a false report is very great indeed.

"Michael, we don't understand many times why some things happen in our lives, why we incur some losses. Many times, however, as the years go by, we do get some understanding and acceptance of blows which at the moment of their happening seem entirely without reason. You have a long life ahead of you. It can be a rich and full one, particularly if you decide that helping, not hurting, others is the way to go.

"Again, let me say you have not only my forgiveness, but my very best wishes for your future."

Governor Reagan expressed his deep belief that there is a divine plan in a letter to a New York woman who had written of her handicapped son. ". . . I find myself believing very deeply that God has a plan for each one of us. Some with little faith and even less testing seem to miss in their mission, or else we perhaps fail to see their imprint on the lives of others. But bearing what we cannot change and going on with what God has given us, confident there is a destiny, somehow seems to bring a reward we wouldn't exchange for any other. It takes a lot of fire and heat to make a piece of steel."

To her son he wrote: ". . . things have a way of working out in life, and usually for the best, if we simply go forward doing our best and trusting that God does have a plan.

"Your handwriting may be 'slow and wiggly,' but already you've conquered this with the typewriter. Your thinking isn't 'slow and wiggly.' All of the miracles we know in this fast-moving world have come from man's brain. Sometimes, some of us have to be forced to use our minds, and we can resent this and grow bitter, or we can go forward, trusting in a divine scheme of things. I think you've made your choice already, and the right one. Your parents must be very proud of you."

Criticism that the governor had no compassion because of some of his welfare policies always bothered him. "Naturally," he said in one letter, "I feel our administration has compassion.

"I'm sure everyone feels sorry for the individual who has fallen by the wayside or who can't keep up in our competitive society, but my own compassion goes beyond that to those millions of unsung men and women who get up every morning, send the kids to school, go to work, try to keep up the payments on their house, pay exorbitant taxes to make possible compassion for the less fortunate, and as a result have to sacrifice many of their own desires and dreams and hopes. Government owes them something better than always finding a new way to make them share the fruit of their toils with others."

The governor also outlined a little of his philosophy of leadership in a letter to Alfred B. Hastings Jr. of Los Angeles. "In this country of ours, we have no titled aristocracy. We do have, of course, a group of people who attain stature and prestige because of accomplishment, not through accident of birth. Our founding fathers, who gave us our start, were men of this kind who had attained stature in their communities and who felt a deep sense of responsibility. I believe their concept of what this country would be was based on a belief that there would always be men of stature who would take time out from their private lives to give service to the community, hold office in government, or contribute in other ways as a kind of repayment for the good fortune they have known. Somewhere along the line, we've lost some of that.

"I believe the time has come for a new noblesse oblige by the American aristocracy of accomplishment."

He concluded: "This country can be as great as the people were willing to make it. But those who have achieved leadership positions in the great private sector owe a little of that leadership to the community as a whole. Politics is too important to be left to politicians. The rewards are indescribable."

In another philosophical letter the governor wrote about an address he made to a group of college-age youth: "I told them probably part of our lack of communication between generations could be a resentment on our part that our sons and daughters seem to assume they and they alone desire peace. I asked them to remember that we, who had bled the finest of our generation into a thousand battlefields around the world in World War II, knew what it was to say good-bye to friends and loved ones. We had a built-in deep love and desire for peace, indeed, a hatred for war. I asked them also to ask themselves what kind of a world they would be living in if our generation had not been willing to do that, if we had not been willing to land on an Omaha Beach or a thousand atolls, or if our young men had not been willing to fight their way across the hedgerows of Normandy or the sands of Africa or up the boot of Italy.

"Each generation must learn that the things men prize the most, the things which make a civilization, are those things for which men have always been willing to die. If our generation has failed, perhaps the failure has been to teach this to our sons and daughters."

Responding to a letter attacking him which appeared in the

Eureka College publication, *Pegasus,* the governor discussed a bit of his philosophy of education: "Education is not the means of showing people how to get what they want. Education is an exercise by means of which enough men, it is hoped, will learn to want what is worth having. Discipline is involved because true freedom of choice is impossible until we are sufficiently self-disciplined to know what the results of our choices will be. A society provides education to assure the continuation of the culture and moral values upon which that society is founded. It is society's attempt to enunciate certain ultimate values upon which individuals and, hence, society may safely build.

"The cynics of ancient Rome challenged every Roman value, derided every standard as middle-class prejudice, and led their students down the path of total rejection and disbelief. They were very successful, as witness the decline and fall of the Roman Empire."

Another letter had this to say about modern education: ". . . today's universities, or at least too many of the faculty, seem bent on regimenting everyone into some kind of forced equality, wherein there will be no reliance on individuals rising above the crowd."

During his years in office the governor gave his views on a wide range of subjects, such as a suggestion that officeholders' tax returns should be made public: "The risk . . . is that more and more, government is tending to pry into the personal lives of citizens and put the information gained on public display. Doing so with elected officials would be a first big step to doing it with everyone, and there goes that issue we fought for in the American Revolution; a citizen has the right of privacy on his books and papers.

"May I add one other drawback? It is hard enough now to get successful and capable people to enter into public life—this could make it almost impossible."

On the subject of bigness: ". . . just being big is not necessarily bad. It is when someone attempts to take advantage of his bigness that we must make sure the smaller fellow is protected against that aggression by superior size and muscle. Strangely enough, many of the people who decry big business . . . are the same ones who justify their lust for big government on the basis that if we're going to have big business and big labor we must have big government.

"Well, I'm opposed to monopoly, whether it be by labor,

88

by business, or by government and I am in favor of a constant three-way attack on those monopolies. ... I believe the biggest threat is big government, but it is supported by and feeds on big labor, and I fear that there are those in business who see a chance at monopoly, whether they use the word or not, if they go along with big government. I'm afraid the fight is never-ending, but we must continue."

On the road to peace: "If you will look back at the periods of the longest peace in our country you will find they have been those times when the United States based its international decisions and relations on sound moral principles with the firm expression that rather than sacrifice such principles we would fight.

"There are those today, I know, who believe in peace at any price. This can only be obtained if you are willing to accept slavery."

And on people-involvement: "In recent years, growing possibly from the great depression years when people were literally stunned by the collapse of the economy, there has been a decline in political participation by the people. The Roosevelt era was characterized by a government takeover to an extent we've never known. Personal initiative was our national characteristic. Organized labor was fragmented and had little power mainly because most Americans resisted joining anything that might restrict their individualism.

"The pattern changed quickly. The year I graduated from college the government was running radio ads urging you not to leave home looking for work, but to stay and wait for the government to help you.

"Today so many things we once thought of as personal or private responsibilities are now just accepted as government's job. With this, in my opinion, has grown the idea that we are incapable as individuals of affecting government. Thus the cliches—'there is no difference between the parties,' 'my vote doesn't count,' and 'politicians are all alike.'

"I have learned that the people can influence government and that our system will only work if the people participate. But the people must be informed, or rather inform themselves.

"Jefferson said the people will not make a mistake—*if* they have *all* the facts. If there is a weakness in our two-party system it is that we accept a party label as ours and then vote the label without questioning whether the party continues to represent our own philosophical beliefs.

"I was a Democrat when the Democratic party stood for states rights, local autonomy, economy in government, and individual freedom. Today it is the party that has changed, openly declaring for centralized federal power and government-sponsored redistribution of the individual's earnings.

"You asked for some ideas. Let me suggest that every government service should be weighed against the cost of that service in loss of personal freedom. We willingly give up our right to drive ninety miles an hour down a city street because we want safety for self and family. By the same token, do we want government to have the right to censor films because some film makers lack good taste?

"Government exists to protect rights which are ours from birth; the right to life, to liberty, and the pursuit of happiness. A man may choose to sit and fish instead of working—that's his pursuit of happiness. He does not have the right to force his neighbors to support him (welfare) in his pursuit because that interferes with their pursuit of happiness."

First and Last Principles

Although Ronald Reagan's interest in national affairs was often labeled "politics" rather than "concern," the truth is that during his governorship, in many ways he became the conscience of our nation because he truly and deeply cares.

Driven by the instincts of a missionary and the perceptions of a student of history who knows that we must heed the lessons of the past if we want to prevent the United States from joining the list of fallen empires, he will continue to be a strong and outspoken voice in America.

The signs of decay and decline in our country today make it plain that we desperately need men of vision, courage, and dedication. The people may not call Ronald Reagan to lead us as president, but I am sure history will record him as one man who strove in perilous times to preserve our country as a great nation.

Ronald Reagan's courage must be unquestioned. He has stood up to the toughest decisions a man in public office must make and not flinched, although, I must say, he has prayed, agonized, and sought the best advice available before deciding.

Few remember the one execution that took place in California when Ronald Reagan was governor. It was early in his administration. The condemned man had killed a policeman in the course of a robbery. Yet there was strong outcry from those opposed to capital punishment. The night before the execution the governor met with his minister and the two men prayed together.

The next morning the governor heard from his legal affairs secretary that there were just no extenuating circumstances, and he ordered the execution to proceed.

At that time there were nearly a hundred men in San Quentin's death row because the governor's predecessor had continually granted stays of execution. A legitimate fear of the governor's was that he would be forced to proceed with the executions of many of them. The Supreme Court ruling against the death penalty, however, took this worry from him. His first execution was also his last. But he remained, and still remains, a strong proponent of the death penalty on the grounds that it is a deterrent to premeditated murder.

Another issue involving life and death with which the governor struggled was abortion. In a letter to Charles Schulz, the creator of Peanuts, Governor Reagan explained his stand. He wrote, he said, because "of one of your strips a few weeks ago which continues to haunt me in a very nice way."

He went on: "Charlie was asking Lucy about what happens to a very nice baby waiting in heaven to be born when the mother and father decide they don't want it. Lucy of course put him down severely. Charlie finished simply remarking he still thought it was a good question.

"Perhaps my feeling for Charlie's question stems from the soul-searching I had to do a few years ago with regard to the liberalizing of our abortion laws. The author of the legislation wanted to go all the way and simply make it a matter of personal choice and wide open. I probably did more studying on that subject at that time than on anything else before or since and finally had to tell him I would veto such a bill. I could only reconcile abortion with the right of self-defense, namely the right of the mother to protect herself and her health against even her own unborn child if the birth of that child threatened her. It has been my feeling that our religion does justify the taking of life in self-defense. I cannot accept that simply on whim even a mother has the right to take the life of her unborn child simply because she thinks that child will be born less than perfect or because she just doesn't want to be bothered. Well, the bill was amended to meet my demands and I signed it into law. Now, however, I have discovered some of our psychiatrists are particularly willing to declare an unwed mother-to-be to have suicidal tendencies, and they do this on a five-minute diagnosis. The result is that our medical program will finance more than fifty thousand abortions of unwed mothers in the coming year on such flimsy diagnosis.

"Well, I didn't mean to let you in on all my problems but just to give the background of why you touched a nerve with your strip the other day. Thanks very much."

Another letter, this to William A. Barker, professor of

physics at the University of California, attested to his strong feelings in this area: "I am deeply committed to a belief in the sacredness of human life. I share your revulsion for the view expressed by your dinner companion that the human fetus is no more than an appendage to be removed as you would an appendix.

"Right now a group of distinguished jurists in the Midwest are seeking a court decision to establish the rights of the unborn child. Their brief cites recent medical research to the effect that an individual, distinct life begins at the moment of conception at which time the genetic components that determine the characteristics of a person are established. Dr. H. M. I. Lilley is quoted as saying, 'The fetus is neither an acquiescent vegetable nor a witless tadpole as some have conceived it to be in the past, but rather is a tiny human being as independent as though lying in a crib with a blanket wrapped around him.'

"I realize there is a body of thought on the other side, but it should follow that where there is doubt as to the question of life or death, the benefit of the doubt should be given to life.

"The California abortion law is based on the Judeo-Christian tradition of self-defense—the right of a woman to take a life in defense of her own. It does not permit the taking of that unborn life simply on the whim of a mother unwilling to carry and bear that child or for fear the child might be born less than perfect.

"Unfortunately, there are those professionals in California, particularly in the field of psychiatry, who are abdicating their responsibility. They are permitting abortions by falsifying as to the mother's risk—claiming self-defense when, in fact, there is no danger. This is as false as claiming self-defense in the murder of a victim who was unarmed and who posed no threat to his killer. You are right to equate this with Hitlerism. How far are we from killing for convenience the unwanted among us if we accept killing them in the womb?"

The governor was dismayed at how the California abortion law was distorted and finally all but rendered void by a ruling of the state supreme court. A letter to Mrs. Win Robinson of Los Angeles displayed his feelings: "California's abortion law *was* based on the rule of self-defense—the right of a woman to protect herself from harm even at the hand of her own unborn child. Provisions for medical review were included in the act to make certain the abortion was necessary to the mother's safety. There is no question but that many, particularly in the field of psychiatry, failed in this responsibility.

"Now the Supreme Court of California has ruled such protective measures need not be applied. I personally think the decision was a license to murder and that we are committing murder on a wholesale scale."

Finally he wrote to Dr. Mildred F. Jefferson of Boston, Massachusetts, a strong opponent of abortion who had appeared on a television show, "The Advocates." "I am disturbed, as you may be, by public-opinion polls showing an almost equal division in the country on this subject. I find it hard to believe that the essentially moral people of this country could in such numbers support abortion on demand unless it is that they are tragically uninformed on the subject.

"I have been meeting with groups of young people in question-and-answer sessions hoping that by such a free exchange they could get a better understanding of government and many of the issues of our time. Invariably, this subject comes up; and here, too, I find that overwhelmingly these young people never give consideration to the human-life aspect but are convinced that abortion is a necessary aid in controlling the birth rate and preventing the birth of unwanted children who will then, according to their belief, live tragic lives.

"I had a touching experience in one such meeting with students from five high schools who had come here to the capitol. One young lady spoke quite eloquently about the fate of the unwanted child after it had been born. I pointed out to them that there were literally millions of people in this country who could not have children and who were lined up waiting, many times for years, to adopt babies that are just not being born now.

"As the session ended, a very pretty, wholesome-looking, fresh-faced young lady sort of tentatively raised her hand; and I took her question as the last that we had time for—I'm glad I did. She said, 'I am adopted. I care very much for my folks; I'm sure they care for me.' And then she added this line. She said, 'I'm glad someone didn't kill me.' I wish we could have that particular little scene on television."

The subject of abortion brings up the subject of birth control and the controversial issue of whether teen-age girls should be prescribed birth control bills or contraceptive devices without parental consent. Here are excerpts of one letter Governor Reagan wrote on the subject to a woman who had told him, "when it comes to an issue such as illegitimacy and avoidance of abortions you make unfortunate decisions and veto legislation designed to lessen illegitimacy and abortions."

". . . what we are really at odds about," the governor responded, "is not finding the solution to the individual's personal tragedy after the mistake has been made and what is the proper course to reduce or hopefully eliminate this cause of the tragedy to begin with.

"I could not have worked in the motion picture industry for most of my adult life and been a 'blue-nose' or prude. Still I have to believe that all law is based on natural law. On the higher law of morality we know that premarital sex or promiscuity in our entire Judeo-Christian tradition is a sin. Most of our common law is based on this concept and belief. In recent years an adult society has said to our young people in a thousand different ways, including the classroom and the lecture hall, that this concept has somehow become outmoded and, therefore, sex ranks with the physical appetites with no more importance assigned to it than eating a ham sandwich when you're hungry. We have, in fact, been preaching or at least accepting hedonism, and not for the first time in man's history. The easy way, of course, is to accept this as a new life-style and adjust accordingly. The more difficult, but I believe proper course dictated by the past, is to return to standards we know are based on solid moral principles. All of history proves that happiness is to be found by following such moral precepts.

"As I said before, I wish I knew the correct answer to all of this. I believe it does lie in education but perhaps the education must begin with the parent. Certainly we have never done a good job in home teaching of our young people about sex. I can't say that I received a scientific dissertation on this at home but on the other hand, I did receive what I now recognize was good, sound moral teaching. You see at close hand the tragedy of the young girl and boy who break the rules and then are faced with the consequences. I see the larger problem of trying to find a way to reverse the hedonism while at the same time having full compassion for those young people who in spite of all teaching are going to make mistakes. How do we do this without seemingly having society put a stamp of approval on hedonism and, in effect, eliminating the notion entirely that the young people have made a mistake? Sex is not a purely physical act. It has deep psychological side effects. It is indeed at the very foundation of our social fabric based on the family unit.

"Part of my resistance also is now based on my view from the inside of government. I think the American people are totally unaware of how dependent they have become on government for making all decisions, regulating even this very intimate facet of family life. Government is not that omnipotent. Government would do a great service for the people if it would unwind its bureaucracy, reduce its size and wean the people and put them back on their own two feet. [I don't mean] that they have to be totally independent of all others but let them find solutions to their problems in such areas as the church, local schools, and Parent-Teacher Associations instead of having them automatically turn to a bureaucrat in some government agency or a legislator in a belief that they can make a determination that will solve all their problems. To sum it up, what problem do we make for the parent who is intelligently trying to teach moral principles to a child when government by way of the school system or whatever agency goes to the contrary and says to the child, 'Here, we know you are going to do these things regardless of what your parents say, so we'll teach you how to get away with it no harm done.' "

Virtually all the problems of human misery and suffering eventually come before any governor of our largest state. Hunger is one of those problems and it is one that is drawing increasing international attention. But like most world problems it is often distorted and seldom understood.

In a letter to Kip Hayden, editor-in-chief of the Eureka College publication, *Pegasus*, Governor Reagan discussed the broad aspects of the problem: "I was very interested in your remarks about the world food situation and the organization you spoke of. I must confess I am not too optimistic about the many world meetings that are being held on hunger. It seems that most of them come up with a very simple, but inadequate answer. The United States representatives sit there, feeling a little guilty because we've been able to feed ourselves, and the rest of the world says, 'Feed us, too.' I realize that many of us have a guilt feeling because, as is so frequently pointed out, the United States has 6 percent of the world's population and consumes 30 percent of the world's goods. This, however, is a misuse of statistics. We also produce 48 percent of the world's goods and our agricultural exploits are the greatest of any nation in the world. The greatest technological revolution in world history hasn't really been in space or any of the other exotic industries, but in American farming. We produce more food for more people with less labor and fewer workers in the field of agriculture than any other nation on earth.

"For many years I have been critical of foreign aid, not because of its intent or goal, but because I believe we have been violating the old admonition that to give a hungry man a fish is to know he'll be hungry tomorrow. To teach him how to fish will insure he'll never be hungry again. Foreign aid over these past decades should have concentrated less on actual food distribution abroad and more on the export of American farming know-how. I still think that is a good idea in the present world situation, although now, of course, we have need for the export of food also, because of the emergency situation in so many areas.

"I have been struck by the absence of national leadership in mobilizing the people of America for efforts that used to be quite commonplace a few decades ago. For example, when the people of America, in a private undertaking but with the cooperation of the national government, saved the starving in Belgium after World War I. A similar effort took place a few years later on the occasion of the Tokyo earthquake, and this was the manner in which people of America went to the aid of others in catastrophes of one kind or another all over the world.

"This brings me to your program of gleaning, such as the corn harvest and then the corn remaining in the field. There are a million opportunities for private saving of food, not only the corn crop, but virtually every harvested crop, particularly the tree crops which leave great amounts that can be gleaned and used to help others.

"But let me point out some other areas. They may sound small, or even a little silly, but I believe there is great potential for saving in them. Four of us had breakfast together in a leading hotel recently and the butter arrived in two dishes, not in the usual pats, but dipped out with ice cream scoops.

97

There was also a basket of bread and toast, etc. No one had asked for this so it was just put on the table as a matter of course. I noted that none of the four of us touched either the butter or the bread. Now, under our health laws, when that is returned from the table it is garbage. It cannot be served to anyone else. Two ice cream scoops of butter and a basket of bread. Would it be too difficult, in this time of shortages, for public eating places to ask first whether bread or butter is desired? Once these things are put on the table, again as I say—and properly so, our health laws require that the food cannot be served to anyone else.

"Banquets are a part of my present job. I've been interested lately to look up and down the head table and note how many times a roll and butter are placed at every setting. I've also noted how few of us eat rolls and butter with our dinner. Again, all that is left must be thrown away.

"I agree with you that we must meet our home problems first. I do disagree that there is widespread hunger in America. This is a fallacy promoted for what reasons I don't know, but actually more than 85 percent of the people of America receive the daily minimum requirement of nutrients, and I am sure that most of the remaining few percent only fail to do so because of ignorance about nutritional standards. This isn't to say there aren't some who fall through the cracks of all of our various programs and do actually experience hunger, and we should continue to do something about this."

The issue of farm labor and particularly Cesar Chavez was a continuing one during the governor's two terms. In one letter the governor wrote, "My position regarding Chavez is well known: the workers must be allowed to vote by secret ballot as to whether they should have a bargaining representative and who or what that representative should be. There can be no morality in either the boycott or in employers and Chavez signing contracts unless and until the workers themselves have voted."

Chavez' efforts to boycott California grapes, wines, and lettuce not handled by his union brought a revealing exchange of correspondence between Governor Reagan and Democratic Governor Milton J. Shapp of Pennsylvania. It began when Shapp, in an effort to help Chavez, issued a directive ordering "all state departments, boards, commissions and agencies [to] cease purchasing Iceburg lettuce."

That directive brought this letter from Reagan:

"Dear Milt:

"A copy of your directive to your state departments ordering them to cease purchasing Iceburg lettuce from Arizona and California has been brought to my attention.

"This comes as a shock to me, especially the statement that 'The United Farm Workers, in their efforts to help seasonal and migrant farm workers to better their conditions have begun a boycott of Iceburg lettuce.'

"I know that a boycott against 'nonunion' lettuce from California was endorsed at the 1972 Democratic presidential nominating convention.

"The truth is that more than 85 percent of all Iceburg lettuce grown in California and Arizona is harvested under union contracts. Only a very small percentage is produced by nonunion workers.

"There are around 170 Teamsters Union contracts in lettuce in the two states, and the United Farm Workers have only four such contracts. All of the Teamsters contracts are as valid as the UFW contracts, and members of the Teamsters Union have far better fringe benefits than do members of UFW.

"The lettuce boycott was inspired by a jurisdictional dispute between Cesar Chavez, who would like to force the growers through a boycott to break their contracts, and the Teamsters Union. Chavez would like all of those contracts turned over to him. For any state to be a party to such a jurisdictional dispute is questionable, to say the least.

"For your information, lettuce crews working in California this year are earning from $5.70 to $7.41 per hour on a piece-rate basis. During the twelve months ending May 31, 1972, farm employees in the Salinas Valley, which grows the biggest part of Iceberg lettuce, averaged $3.07 per hour. This was a composite average of piece rates, hourly, and hourly plus incentive-pay rates, with hourly guarantee jobs, and did not include foremen or salaried workers.

"The U.S. Department of Labor has recommended to all the states ten protective laws for farm workers. California has nine of those laws in effect, and the same table indicates that Pennsylvania has only six.

"The average pay of all hired farm workers in California

in April of this year was $2.27 per hour; Pennsylvania's average farm-worker pay in 1971 was $1.68 per hour.

"From these facts, it would appear that Pennsylvania should be concerned about its own farm workers rather than taking punitive action against California's lettuce growers and workers, who enjoy the best working conditions for farm workers in the United States.

"It would be more appropriate to undertake a greater degree of cooperation among states rather than to engage in this dispute."

Governor Shapp replied:

"Dear Ron:

"I have read with a great deal of interest your letter of September 27th asking me in effect to mind my own business in regard to the attempts of Cesar Chavez to gain fair treatment for his people.

"This is exactly what I am doing. I am minding my own business.

"As an individual, I am greatly disturbed by the plight of the poor people in this nation, and the oppressive forces that keep them down.

"As a governor, I am trying to do something to help solve the social and economic ills that beset my state and the nation so that the American dream can be fulfilled not just by a comparative handful of wealthy people, but by all our citizens.

"Lettuce today has replaced grapes as a symbol, just as grapes at one time had quietly replaced the 'union label' as a symbol for obtaining fair treatment for labor.

"Cesar Chavez is attempting to accomplish for his people what Eugene Debs did for the railroad workers, what John L. Lewis did for the miners, what Philip Murray did for the steelworkers, what Dubinsky did for the needle trade workers, what Samuel Gompers did for the cigar makers, what Walter Reuther did for the auto workers, and yes, what James Hoffa did for the truck drivers. All of these great labor leaders gave the working men and women of America a chance to work under safe conditions, at fair wages, and to be treated with dignity.

"Throughout its turbulent history, the labor movement in America has always been opposed by those who have considered material values more important than human values.

"At one time in your career you were part of the move-

100

ment to help those at the bottom reach out for daylight. But once you achieved personal success, you seemed to have changed. That was your privilege.

"But it is still my privilege to do my job as I see it.

"I believe strongly that this nation cannot achieve the goals it espouses until and unless its leaders work to help all the people, not just the privileged few.

"I believe strongly that it is your responsibility as a governor, just as it is mine, to use all the powers at our disposal to constantly fight to correct the wrongs that exist within our society to the end that this nation can indeed exist under God, with liberty and justice for all.

"Perhaps this may sound kind of corny to some, but it never sounds corny to me when I pledge allegiance to our flag.

"Pennsylvania farmers are not being harmed by the boycott of Iceburg lettuce. They are being helped to the extent that they have a greater opportunity to sell native-grown lettuce to our institutions.

"But more importantly, if all Pennsylvania citizens join with the millions of other Americans to support the present effort of Cesar Chavez, then all our people will benefit because another group of the downtrodden will be helped in the untiring effort to achieve a dignified way of life for all people.

"Ron, I shall continue to do my job as I see it—to fight constantly to help all Pennsylvania citizens obtain greater value from government for their tax dollars, to promote consumer-oriented programs, and to improve the quality of life for all our citizens.

"We have great financial and material resources in this nation, and we have great human talent.

"There is nothing that the leaders of this nation cannot accomplish for our people once we stop giving lipservice to our oft-stated principles and put our hearts and muscles behind humanely oriented, realistic programs.

"I'll mind my business in Pennsylvania. Good luck to you in California."

And this brought a last response from Governor Reagan:

"Dear Milt:

"I was touched by your eloquent and moving letter; so much so that I would like to offer a constructive suggestion.

"First, however, so that you'll have no question as to my

sincere interest, may I correct a misapprehension on your part? You indicated a belief that while I had served the cause of organized labor for a time, my views changed to the point of losing my capacity for compassion as I became 'better off.'

The Screen Actors Guild (an AFL-CIO union) has a proud tradition of service to its members by working actors who for the most part have a certain individual bargaining power and really don't need union representation. Among those who have served as president were Eddie Cantor, Jimmy Cagney, Robert Montgomery, George Murphy, Walter Pidgeon, and Charlton Heston, to name a few.

"My own six terms as president were during a time when I had achieved stardom and was probably at the height of my career and my earning power.

"As I pointed out in my last letter, 85 percent of California lettuce is presently harvested by unionized labor (International Teamsters) and the salary scale is somewhat higher here than in other states. I'm sure you would like to see all the states reach parity with California.

"My suggestion therefore is that you persuade the agriculture industry of your state to invite Cesar Chavez to come and organize the farm workers of Pennsylvania. This is a sacrifice California is prepared to make in the interest of human compassion and I assure you, thousands of our own farm workers—particularly those citizens of Mexican heritage—will courageously, and I might even say happily, carry on without him.

"Your own citizens will once again enjoy the taste of Iceburg lettuce from California and Californians will feel the urge to purchase the products of Pennsylvania."

The governor sent a copy of his first letter to Shapp to Governor Jack Williams of Arizona, which inspired a note in return:

"Dear Ron:

"Really appreciated your letter of September 27th addressed to our dear friend The Honorable Milton J. Shapp.

"It occurs to me that if we're going to start this interesting exercise, Arizona and California should begin boycotting social workers, Vista workers, Ph.D's, dangerous insects, and other such items crossing our state line from Pennsylvania.

"I should imagine at this point William Penn is revolving rapidly in his grave.

"Best regards."

Another governor, Robert Ray of Iowa, sent Reagan a clipping of a news story which reported that "the Texas Senate voted a resolution of praise for farm worker organizer Cesar Chavez."

Reagan wrote back: "Thanks very much for sending me the clipping about Cesar Chavez and the Texas Senate. It makes me realize how true is the old saying, 'No man's life or property is safe while the legislature is in session.'

"Why do you suppose it is that we just never will ask those who have been there. We've had several years of Mr. Chavez here in California, and we find he neither represents the people he claims to represent, nor does he apparently have any intention of bettering their lot, and certainly he is not nonviolent. His terror tactics easily match those of the old-time night riders in the South. Incidentally, he's the only man I've ever known who can go on a fast and gain weight.

"Last spring in an effort to resolve this situation out here, I offered the state's help in holding, once and for all, secret ballot elections whereby the workers in the fields could vote on whether they wanted union representation and if so which union. The workers were in favor, the farmers agreed to abide by the decision, and the holdout that made it impossible was Cesar Chavez.

"When the grape boycott was at its height, and some mayors like our own John Lindsay were joining the boycott, I issued invitations to mayors all over the country to come to California as our guests and see for themselves. The only one who accepted the invitation was the young mayor of Vancouver, British Columbia. They're fairly well socialized there and he evidently leaned that way, including a bias toward Chavez. But he arrived, went into the fields, met with the workers in the fields, traced every rumor and story for himself, and walked down the picket lines. After four days he told the press of California there would be no boycott of grapes in his city. He said he had found no workers in the fields who wanted to join Chavez's union and he found no pickets on the picket lines who were farm workers.

"Well, this is little thanks for your good letter to make you put up with such a diatribe. As you've guessed, I've had my fill of Mr. Chavez and now I've had my fill of the Texas Senate. Spare both our states from such."

A former governor with whom Governor Reagan had occasion to correspond was his predecessor, Edmund G. "Pat"

Brown, Sr. Brown, although known as an amiable man, has always resented his defeat at the hands of an "actor" and the bitterness shows through from time to time. A Republican fundraising letter signed by the governor was sent to Brown by mistake. This kind of mistake is common when computerized mass mailings are used, but the former governor took the opportunity to respond snidely. The fundraising letter made another mistake common to computers and addressed him as "Dear Hon. Brown:" because it was addressed to Hon. (instead of Mr.) Edmund G. Brown and the computer was programmed to pick up the title and the last name.

Brown wrote back:

"Dear Hon. Reagan:

"In today's mail I received a letter from you recalling the days of the Brown-Unruh clique.

"I am very interested in your record of increased taxation, increased welfare costs, and property taxes.

"I really believe that Edmund G. Brown, Jr. will do a far better job than your hand-picked candidate, Houston Flournoy. I must, therefore, refuse your kind invitation to contribute to the Republican State Central Committee.

"Sincerely,

"Edmund G. Brown"

Chuckling all the while, the governor penned a short reply:

"Dear Pat:

"I just thought you might be ready to do penance."

As he points out from time to time, Governor Reagan was active in his own union, the Screen Actors Guild, in which he served six terms as president. Even so, many conservatives are surprised when they discover he is not a strong advocate of right-to-work laws. Many union members are also surprised. In a letter to David Y. Denholm, executive assistant to the president of Californians for Right to Work, Reagan explained: "You and I are in agreement about many things with regard to the rights of rank-and-file union members which must be protected. At the same time, however, my own experience as a union member, officer, and several times president, has convinced me these matters can be corrected within the union shop framework. (You'll note I didn't say closed shop.)"

But, although a believer in unionism, the governor is an even stronger believer in less government interference in the private sector and in "the coercive redistribution of wealth."

He writes in a letter to George L. Browning of Van Nuys, California, "The less government that I advocate . . . refers to the flood of restrictive regulations spawned by recent congressional acts which have added, for example, paperwork to the small businessmen of America that requires some 130 million man-hours at a cost of $50 billion simply to fill out government forms which then are shuffled and reshuffled in Washington at another expense of some $20 billion. I have no intention of suggesting that we eliminate those time-tested regulations which are necessary to protect us from the unscrupulous—for example, the pure food laws. . . .

"You suggest it is bigotry to criticize those practices of socialist or communist countries. I believe the danger of people in America getting the idea such practices might be good here requires a warning that a loss of individual freedom we've never experienced would go with the adoption of such practices. I am opposed also to the coercive redistribution of wealth in our free economy by government fiat. On the other hand, I have, in a number of speeches, advocated a distribution based on our capitalistic practice that there are ways to increase the ownership of our industry to the point that the majority of our workers could have not only their salary but the income derived from sharing ownership in the industries in which they work. I believe there are ways, and I have suggested some, where this could be done without taking away that which someone else owns.

"As for the unmet needs in our society which you referred to, all of those I think can better be met by a general increase in the productivity of our land and in a broader-based prosperity than through the bureaucracy of government.

"The cooperation of government, of industry, and of labor to find a way in which capitalism can be made more general, with the bulk of our people participating in individual ownership—not the collective ownership by way of government that is advocated by some and practiced in some countries—is necessary."

His opposition to a particular tax proposition on the 1972 ballot brought many letters of protest. In response to one he declared: "The plain truth is, for many, many years we have all been lied to about taxing business and thus reducing the individual's tax burden. There is no way that business can be made to pay a tax. Business collects taxes, and if businesses cannot include all of their taxes as production expenses in the price of their product, they go out of business. There are 116 business taxes, so-called, in the price of a suit of clothes. All such taxes are passed on to the ultimate consumer—the individual citizen. The real problem with taxes in our country is simply the high cost of government, and taxes cannot be lowered until the people hold government more accountable. Now, who is the real villain in that picture? Out of your tax dollar the federal government gets seventy cents. The state government is run on about seven cents of that dollar, and the rest goes for schools and local and county governments."

The prospect of adding regional governments at either the federal or state levels is a real concern to many Americans. The governor answered one letter on this subject, in part: "The president [Nixon] from the first has sought to decentralize the Washington bureaucrats and get more authority and decision-making back to state and local governments. To this end he regionalized a number of federal agencies to lessen decision-making in Washington and to give the states an ability to resolve issues without taking on the Washington bureaucracy."

For his own part, he said, ". . . while I recognize there will be problems mutual to several communities, it is my belief any regional approach to those problems should be made by the elected representatives of those communities. I do not favor the creation of any additional layer of government."

The energy crisis also brought letters and responses. To Maxwell H. Smith of Malibu, California, he wrote: "I think before we tee off on the oil industry itself, we had better look at the record regarding warnings coming from that industry about this present shortage. In 1960 the American Association of Petroleum Geologists met at a convention in Los Angeles and predicted that by 1975 the United States would be in exactly the situation we're in now. They added these words, 'When it happens they will blame the industry and say, why didn't you warn us; well, we're warning you now.'

"As to the other matter, for a long time I have firmly believed the answer to all our waste problems was finding a use for them. It's all well and good to post signs saying do not litter, but if the litter becomes too valuable to throw away the problem is solved. I think you will be reassured to know that we have a pilot plant right now that has discovered that it can make oil from garbage. A little more atmosphere-polluting than petroleum, but still an oil than can be used, perhaps where pollution is not such a problem. We also have discovered, and are running a pilot plant, making oil from the rice hulls we used to burn. What is even more exciting, I think, is the discovery that we can convert sludge and decaying garbage to methane gas which can be used to generate electricity.

"I think the Arabs did us a favor by bringing the issue to a head; they didn't cause our problems for we were on our way to this shortage even with their oil, but now perhaps we'll go forward and find the other fuel sources that will make all our throwaways useful."

The governor occasionally answered letters addressed to his wife on pertinent governmental issues. One had to do with amnesty. "I hope you won't mind my answering your letter to Mrs. Reagan, but it just seemed simpler for me to write rather than relay the information through her," he wrote. And continued: "Very simply it boils down to this: we are a nation governed by law, not men. This is the great protector of our freedom, in contrast to the days of kings (or modern-day dictators) wherein a ruler decided for or against someone by his own whim. With our freedom, of course, goes a responsibility to see that the law is upheld.

"In this case the law requires that we all serve our country when the duly-elected government decides the national policy requires such service. There has never been a war in our history when *all* our citizens agreed with the government's decision, yet the majority always abided by the law, knowing that we cannot have an orderly society if individuals can pick and choose the laws they will obey.

"Today some people are saying that because some young men considered the war immoral and avoided the draft or deserted, they should be able to return to America with no penalty now that the war is over. This, of course, is to say they should be allowed to break the law without fear of penalty.

"It is also being said that we have always granted such amnesty after previous wars. This is not true. Dating back to President Washington and the 'Whiskey Rebellion,' there has *never* been an unconditional amnesty for draft dodgers or deserters."

After tracing the record of amnesty grants by various presidents, the governor concluded: "If today's deserters are willing to return acknowledging their guilt, willing to stand

107

trial and accept the court's decision, then amnesty could be granted on an individual basis, just as it is granted at times to other types of lawbreakers."

The United States' positions on two small foreign nations have been controversial over the years. Regarding Israel, Governor Reagan wrote to Mr. and Mrs. D. E. Matus of Glendale, California: "I believe the United States is *and should be* committed to the preservation of Israel. I am convinced this is the policy of the Nixon administration. Indeed, I have been informed this is so.

"Let me sum up the Middle East situation as I believe it is and has been. Israel, outnumbered one hundred to one in the population of unfriendly surrounding nations, has held its own with the help of American military supplies. In addition, the United States presence in the area has kept the Soviet Union outside the Middle East, at least as an active participant. If ever the United States gave up that role, it wouldn't make much difference whether or not we supplied arms to Israel.

"Since the ceasefire, the president has enlarged the role of the United States. He has moved boldly to befriend the Arab states and replaced the Soviet influence in those countries. I think the reaction of the Arabs has made it plain they were uncomfortable in their relations with Russia. This move puts the United States in a position of being able to influence the Arabs and act as an intermediary and a friend of both sides. Frankly, I believe it has been a brilliant policy, brilliantly carried out."

After Taiwan, the Republic of China, was ousted from the United Nations, the governor wrote directly to President and Madame Chiang Kai-chek, whom the Reagans had visited earlier on a mission for President Nixon:

"Mrs. Reagan and I want you to know how deeply shocked and disappointed we were by the completely immoral action of the U.N. General Assembly.

"I have told the President of my displeasure at what can only be described as the moral bankruptcy of an organization now reduced to the level of a kangaroo court."

The Captain of a Family

It's been said that nobody really knows Ronald Reagan. While he is an open, warm, and thoughtful individual, he is also an intensely private man. I suspect that his being in the public eye since almost from the time he was graduated from college has something to do with his trying to preserve what little privacy he can. But the air of dignity he lent to his office was certainly a factor in imparting that feeling of aloofness. He was always the governor; never one of the boys. A Ronald Reagan in a smoke-filled rap session after hours with his staff, or political friends, sitting behind the desk with rolled up shirt sleeves, open collar, feet on his desk, is as inconceivable to me as is the possibility that he might ever have been engaged in political shenanigans and intrigue. Of course he inherited an Irish temper and I must admit to having caught him using four-letter words. While they are in the mild category and wouldn't shock most people, he will blush and utter an embarrassed apology on catching himself.

It's been sheer pleasure to work for him, but it's my turn to be embarrassed when asked by my friends about what type of a man he is. When I tell the truth—which I feel I must—I sound like a propaganda agent, for who today believes there is a public servant among us who is everything we can ever hope to find: honest, dedicated, concerned, possessing both wisdom and foresight. Yet he truly has these qualities.

Home, with his wife and family, is the governor's favorite place. That's where he is happiest and relaxes the best. He adores and admires Nancy, his wife, and is a good friend and father to his children. The letters included in this section reveal much about Ronald Reagan's relationship with his family. They will tell you more about him than any story I might relate.

Lately, much has been said about political couples; the strains of office invariably take their toll. But Ronald and

Nancy Reagan are a shining exception. They have shown that no occupation must automatically be a threat to a husband-wife relationship if there is sufficient love and understanding. It cannot be easy on any wife having to share her husband with twenty-one million constituents, but I'm certain Nancy Reagan never felt neglected, because he never allowed business to push her to the background. At the time, she fully understood her husband's responsibilities and took a great interest in what he was doing. Although she was careful never to interfere with his official duties, she was—and is—not afraid to speak her mind if she felt the staff pushed the governor too hard. The Reagans are totally devoted to each other. They have shared all the triumphs and defeats of his political career.

The governor has never been embarrassed about showing or writing about his love for Nancy. In a letter to Gregory C. Kimberlin, head of a Los Angeles community health center, he wrote: "I hope you all know how very sorry I am that I can't be with you today. Would you please tell your guest of honor that I will be calling on her when I get back to California, at which time I'll express my heartfelt appreciation for the effort she has put forth in this worthy cause as well as others.

"I have long admired her and upon my return to California intend not only to tell her that, but also that I love her more than anyone in the whole wide world."

It is only as the letter ends that you realize he is talking about Nancy. That was in 1974.

But in 1971 he received a request from Helen Gurley Brown, editor of *Cosmopolitan*, asking him to jot down "the nicest thing a girl ever did for me."

The governor responded: "The nicest thing a girl ever did for me was when a girl named Nancy married me and brought a warmth and joy to my life that has grown with each passing year."

His sense of humor, which he often has to fight to keep from showing, came through in this letter, however, and he continued: "I know she won't mind if I say the second nicest thing was a letter from a little fifth grade girl last week. She added a P.S., 'You devil you.' I've walked with a swagger ever since."

The governor's children also have occupied an important place in his life. They were among the reasons the Reagans

110

refused to live in the old governor's mansion when they first went to Sacramento. Not only was the house a firetrap but there was no place for the younger children to play and no neighboring homes which would provide playmates for the children.

When his son, Michael Reagan, was getting married the governor sent him a letter that expressed his own belief in the sacredness of the marriage vows:

"Dear Mike:

"Enclosed is the item I mentioned (with which goes a torn up IOU). I could stop here but I won't.

"You've heard all the jokes [that have] been rousted around by all the 'unhappy marrieds' and cynics. Now, in case no one has suggested it, there is another viewpoint. You have entered into the most meaningful relationship there is in all human life. It can be whatever you decide to make it.

"Some men feel their masculinity can only be proven if they play out in their own life all the locker-room stories, smugly confident that what a wife doesn't know won't hurt her. The truth is, somehow, way down inside, without her ever finding lipstick on the collar or catching a man in the flimsy excuse of where he was till 3 A.M., a wife does know, and with that knowing, some of the magic of this relationship disappears. There are more men griping about marriage who kicked the whole thing away themselves than there can ever be wives deserving of blame. There is an old law of physics that you can only get out of a thing as much as you put in. The man who puts into the marriage only half of what he owns will get that much out. Sure, there will be moments when you will see someone or think back on an earlier time when you will be challenged to see if you can still make the grade, but let me tell you how really great is the challenge of proving your masculinity and charm with one woman for the rest of your life. Any man can find a twerp here and there who will go along with cheating and it doesn't take all that much manhood. It does take quite a man to remain attractive and be loved by a woman who has heard him snore, seen him unshaven, tended him while he was sick, and washed his dirty underwear. Do that and keep her still feeling a warm glow and you will know some very beautiful music. If you truly love a girl, you shouldn't ever want her to feel, when she sees you greet a secretary or a girl you both know, that humiliation of wondering if she was someone who caused you to be

111

late coming home, nor should you want any other woman to be able to meet your wife and know she was smiling behind her eyes as she looked at her, the woman you love, remembering this was the woman you rejected even momentarily for her favors.

"Mike, you know better than many what an unhappy home is and what it can do to others. Now you have a chance to make it come out the way it should. There is no greater happiness for a man than approaching a door at the end of a day knowing someone on the other side of that door is waiting for the sound of his footsteps.

"Love, Dad

"P.S. You'll never get in trouble if you say 'I love you' at least once a day."

The governor's younger son is named Ronald, also, but he is not a junior because he does not have his dad's middle name, Wilson. The Reagans nicknamed him "the Skipper." In late 1969 the governor took him to see the Los Angeles Rams professional football team play in the Los Angeles Coliseum. Following the game, he took Skipper to the dressing room to meet the Rams players. Afterward the following exchange of correspondence took place.

"Dear Governor Reagan:

"It was nice to see you after the game Sunday even if the occasion wasn't a happy one.

"I hope that Skipper got a few autographs and that he enjoys the game football.

"With all good wishes.

"Most sincerely,

"George Allen

"P.S. I'm checking on pads and helmet for Skipper and will send."

"Dear George:

"I had intended to write you but now can write and answer your kind letter. I'm most grateful to you for your help on the pads and helmet and want you to understand I didn't mean to be a freeloader on this. So please send a bill for whatever you are able to do.

"Now let me tell you about what that Sunday afternoon and the visit to the dressing room meant. This was our first chance to see the team other than by way of TV. We are all fans and the Skipper, I think, lives and dies with the Rams.

112

He was, of course, greatly disappointed by the outcome of the game. You and I know, however, that defeats must be borne with the victories. But in the stands around us were those few to be found in any crowd—the fellows who wanted to talk about their beliefs that the pros shaved points to benefit the gamblers. Then there were other voices raised about, 'Well, they don't need this game, so they are not really making an effort.' With all that cynicism, particularly among those who have never been on the field themselves, I just want you to know that I walked out of that dressing room with my feet off the ground. To stand there with an eleven-year-old boy when his heroes dropped to their knees in prayer was something I'll never forget and for which I will always be grateful.

"Nothing a father could tell his son would ever match the impact of that moment. In spite of my own playing days and the years later as a sports announcer, I must confess to my surprise at that moment. But, it was a happy and thrilling surprise.

"Again, as I say, I don't know whether the fellows will ever know what that meant. I hope you don't mind that I've been giving some circulation among our friends to this experience, and it's been a most effective Christmas story.

"We'll be watching on the 27th and, if the power of positive thinking exists, you'll have two extra men on the field—me and the Skipper.

"Please give my best to all the men on the team.

"Sincerely,

"Ronald Reagan

"P.S. As far as I am concerned, California has no finer representatives or better ambassadors than the Rams."

The governor also wrote to the Rams' quarterback, Roman Gabriel, saying, in part, "I just wanted you to know how much I appreciate your kindness to him in the dressing room, but more than that, how very much the entire afternoon meant to me as a father. I'm referring to the impact on an eleven-year-old when he saw his heroes on their knees in prayer. I don't think any words of mine or any lecturing could ever match what this meant and the effect it had on him. And I couldn't begin to express what it meant to me to have him share that experience."

The governor also had occasion to write to the Skipper while he was attending Webb School in Claremont, Califor-

113

nia. Many a father has had the opportunity, or rather the responsibility, of writing this kind of letter to his own son:

"Dear Son:

"This letter may ramble a bit because it has to do with some concerns of mine. I suppose they are concerns every father has as he watches his son go through each year and period of life that he himself went through and remembers so much more clearly than you might think the opportunities he missed and the needless mistakes he made.

"Some fathers get so uptight in their concern they wind up trying to relive their own youth by stage-directing their son's life. I hope by now I've convinced you this is not my intention or desire. Some fathers cop out and, under the pretense of being a 'pal,' don't set any ground rules at all, and thus avoid having to make any tough decisions. This I have no intention of doing.

"These concerns have been on my mind for some time, and so has this letter. Now it has been triggered by your report card. You did fine in Ancient History—B+. You also had a B+ in English I, but an unsatisfactory effort. This makes the B+ less to be desired than a lower grade if the lower grade represented the absolute best effort of which you were capable. But then comes a lesser grade, a C— in French I, with a notation that, 'The quality of work has diminished quite a bit.' Again I say the C— would be all right with me if it represented your best try. This would be true also of the D in Algebra I, but the effort was rated unsatisfactory and the teacher's notation read, 'Ron has been relying on last year too long—he'd better force himself to get to work or he'll be in trouble.'

"Everything in life has a price and our biggest mistakes are when we don't really ask the price before we make our choice. Do you remember our Christmas shopping and the jolt you had when you had the gift wrapped and then heard the price?

"The 'trouble' the algebra teacher mentioned is the price you pay for not forcing yourself to work at something that is less interesting than other things you'd rather do. For example, the price can be ineligibility for outside activities, including athletics. It can be cancellation of summer plans because you have to make up credits in summer school. It can be limitation of your choice of colleges because you don't meet the requirements of the ones you'd really like. It can even be taking five years to get through school instead of four, and actually it can be all of these, which is quite a price to pay for a little goofing off.

"This period of the school year, whether it be high school or college, is the toughest. Don't ask me why, but it's always been true. This is when the excitement of fall and starting the new year seems a long way back and the summer an even longer way ahead. It's easy to get bored, to complain about everything and to think the school and everyone connected with it are out to ruin your life. This is when you have to remember the price for giving up and copping out. It's also the time when you build some character muscle to see you through real problems that come along later in life. And they do come along.

"It's only a few years now (they seem many to you) until you'll be out of school and really beginning your life. All that has gone before and these remaining few years of school and college are 'spring training' for the real season. When we are young we look at adults going about their day-to-day work and it all seems pretty dull and uninteresting. Believe me, that isn't so. I can't remember a time since graduation when I've been bored. Finding the thing you want to do and making a go of it is next in importance to finding the person you want to share your life with.

"Here again what you do now affects the choices you have. When I was announcing sports I was happy and thought that was all I wanted out of life. Then came the chance at Hollywood and that was even better. Now I'm doing something that makes everything else I've done seem dull as dishwater when I look back. But without some of the things I had to learn in college and didn't particularly care about, without some of the chores I didn't like when I was doing the G.E. television show, I couldn't do and wouldn't have had the chance to do what I'm doing now.

"We don't know what turns our life will take or what doors will open and there is nothing worse than to have such a door open and then learn you gave away your admittance ticket back in your school days.

"The other day when we were talking about the POWs we spoke of self-discipline and how it saved their lives. There is an inner man within all of us we have to call on once in a while. Having the guts to do the nasty little boring tasks, sticking to them when we'd rather goof off, decides whether

115

that inner man has enough muscle to be of any help when we need him.

"Six months ago in the graduating class of the California Highway Patrol Academy there was a young man who led the class. He really wanted a career in the patrol and being top man in that class took a lot of doing, both in the brain and the muscle departments. A couple of weeks ago on the San Bernardino Freeway a drunk driver hit him and sheared his right leg off below the knee. Can you imagine what life looked like to him and his young wife? Oh sure, he'd get a pension, he wouldn't starve, but what would he do with his life besides sit on the front porch? Well, it won't be that way. He bought more than that with his willingness to put out at the academy. We are going to break the old rules and when he's up and on an artificial leg we are putting him back on duty as a patrolman. Now he has a double job—he has a chance if he makes it to open the door for others who suffer disabling injuries so they won't wind up in a rocker on the front porch. Think of the price he might be paying now if he'd decided to be just another kid 'getting by' when he was in the academy.

"Well, if you've read this far let me just wrap it up by telling you your mother and I have known many moments of great pride in you. We've also known moments of doubt in ourselves; times when we've worried as to whether we've made that inner man as strong as he'll need to be sometime later in life when you call on him for help.

"Keep an eye on the price tag; some things are very expensive and you pay for the rest of your life."

Governor Reagan, of course, wrote many letters to friends as well as to total strangers during his days in office. Once, for instance, he received a letter from a well known actress and close friend who wrote that "my husband and I are house hunting. We love our present home, but we are literally being forced out of it by those darned 'movie-star maps.'

"Aside from having our doorbell rung at odd hours (once at 5 A.M., TRUE!), the cars line up in front of the house and people jump out and grab at the kids when they come home from school. Also, people in our profession are prime targets for robbers. Especially when it's announced we're out of town.

116

"So—we're moving. Still, I'm afraid that once we're settled in a new home, the same thing will start all over, after awhile. Maybe Arizona *is* the answer.

"I'm writing you because you, of all people, can certainly understand the problem.

"Is there *any* way of outlawing these maps and the people who sell them?

"I love my profession, and I love the public, but I *do* feel we are all entitled to the privacy of our home.

"Thank you for reading this, and any suggestions or leads you can give me will certainly be appreciated."

The governor replied:

"How I wish I could write a letter answering your problem. Unfortunately, there is no answer except the heartbreaking one you, yourselves, have found, which is to move. Evidently the law is such that records of addresses are open to public view and there is no way to prevent someone from pointing out a house and telling others who lives there. For what it's worth, let me tell you of my own experience some years ago.

"I discovered the buses were still stopping and identifying a house as mine from which I had long ago moved. It was then I learned that the houses must be within an area the buses can cover within a limited period of time. We had moved to the Palisades, and that was too far out for them, so they just kept on stopping at the same house. I don't know what your plans are or whether you have found a new home as yet, but it is something to think about. I believe Beverly Hills, Brentwood, and Bel Air, are probably the danger zones.

"Again, I wish I could have sent a better and more satisfying answer. Nancy sends her best. We are still both watching and enjoying."

He also wrote to a total stranger—a newborn baby boy, the following:

"Dear Ronald:

"Welcome to the world. You'll probably have to ask who this other Ronald is by the time you can read this and the answer is, he's just someone who is highly honored that your parents chose his name for you.

"Some people will try to tell you this world you've come into is a pretty sick place. Don't you believe it. It's filled with wonderful people like your parents and this country is the

117

best part of that world so believe in it, serve it as best you can and love your fellow man.

"Sincerely,

"Ronald Reagan"

An emotional exchange of correspondence took place between the governor and the Reverend James E. Jones, pastor of Westminster Presbyterian Church in Los Angeles. The governor's reply again shows his reliance on the Lord.

The Reverend Jones wrote:

"Dear Mr. Reagan,

"In the spring of 1969 as president of the Los Angeles Unified School District I led a delegation of teachers up to Sacramento to discuss with you surplus dollars for schools and the cost of living and not tax refunds. Our request to see you was denied. Other controversial school matters produced in me great annoyance and resentment towards you as a person. Further, I even blamed you for my defeat April 1969 when really the Lord knew my task on that board was finished. It was during the roasting of Bob Hope that God showed me my error, for you were having a great time that evening being truly 'human.' Then the night you gave your testimony at Coronado for the Laymen's Leadership Institute I knew that if I was to be really free I had to ask that you find it in your heart to forgive me. Strange that such a thing should stay on my heart, but this is the way the Spirit works. I trust that you will forgive the error of my way. I told Don Moomaw that such was so. Wherever you go, whatever you do rest assured that my blessings and prayers go with you."

And the governor replied:

"Dear Reverend Jones:

"From the bottom of my heart I thank you for your letter. There are no words to express what it means to me.

"In these past several years when frustrations built up it was very easy to be filled with bitterness and resentment amounting almost to hate. I don't know when the realization came to me of how inconsistent it was to ask God's help at the same time I was hating my brothers—his children.

"My most frequent prayer now is for forgiveness and help in conquering anger and bitterness. Oh, I can't claim total success but I'm trying. Your letter will make it much easier for me and for that I thank you."

The Ogre in Sacramento

Actually, it is this chapter which prompted me to want to publish the Reagan letters in the first place. Few men are as compassionate and as inherently kindly as the governor. That only a relatively few people seem to be aware of these traits can be blamed on his relentless opposition—those professional politicians and do-gooders—who see his fiscal responsibility and the courage he exhibited in cracking down on criminals and welfare chiselers as heartlessness towards the poor, the sick, and the old.

How very unfair!

Admittedly, of course, Ronald Reagan is not the only victim of such oratory. It's a stigma the liberals incessantly and successfully attach to conservatives, while claiming for themselves a monopoly of "concern for the little people." But since when can a man's feeling toward his fellow man be judged by his political or governmental philosophy?

Just because the governor demanded accountability from all government programs, including such sacred institutions as the University of California and the mental health program, just because he felt certain areas are better handled by the private sector, must this mean he doesn't identify with the people's desires and dreams and hopes, and doesn't care about their health, their education, and their welfare?

It's a convenient, demagogic accusation which, unfortunately, has created the myth that the Republicans in general and the governor in particular are insensitive to the people's needs and desires.

Having observed at firsthand for eight years one of these "cold, out-for-the-rich" Republicans, I find the situation ironic, to say the least. I am convinced that it would be impossible for any person with matching responsibilities to become more involved and be more sympathetic to individual hardship cases than was Governor Reagan.

Unfortunately, the best examples are not confined to one or two letters for easy publication in this chapter. There is no way in which I could adequately describe his interest in the well-being of two women, both in their fifties, who live on the meager state's contribution to their brother—a cerebral palsy victim. While it is true that their plight is self-imposed because they sternly refuse to commit "Buzzy" to the institution in which he rightfully belongs, the governor has never questioned their decision to honor their mother's deathbed request to personally take care of their unfortunate brother. The governor was genuinely touched when he received a letter from them a couple of years ago in which they told their sad story—that they couldn't get enough home work to sustain themselves even though they are skilled leather craftsmen and experienced writers, willing and able to take on any size order or work. What prompted them to write the governor was an administrative technicality which caused the loss of an increase in their brother's income on which they had counted to finally fill Buzzy's greatest wish: a rocking chair. Although the governor could not change state regulations and grant the increase, he so sympathized with their situation that he sent his own rocking chair. When he brought it into the office for shipping, our "don't you use it yourself" intervention brought a simple, "yeah, but this poor guy needs it more than I."

That was the beginning of a correspondence which expanded into an exchange of about a hundred letters in three years. What do they have to tell each other? Well, this unlikely relationship has developed out of a sense of sponsorship on the governor's part toward those three lonely people who are almost completely cut off from society and whose only complaint—despite severe hardships—has been a lack of opportunity to work.

The governor has been determined to do what he can to help them—so far with only limited success. But the fact that he tried and never gave up had a heartwarming and lasting effect on our whole staff. Here was the governor of the most populous state in the union, faced with a multitude of problems and pressures, talking to friends and visiting quality leathergoods stores in Beverly Hills like a traveling salesman, showing off Bertha and Sam's really magnificent craftsmanship and soliciting orders. At the same time, he personally wrote a number of small-town papers that he thought might be interested in starting a daily column with the sisters' folksy, but perceptive wisdom and humor.

Their several published books on California's colorful heritage have also been submitted to a movie producer. The governor is an eternal optimist and believer in our country's system and people. He knows that somehow, sometime, this family will find financial security, thus justifying his faith in our country's heritage of opportunity for all who are willing to work for it.

In late 1974 the sisters made a leather belt for former President Nixon and asked the governor to send it to him. Along with the belt went a note from the governor which said:

"Let me explain a little about this gift from 'Miss Sam and Miss Bertha.' I have never met them, but we have had a steady correspondence for about two years now. It all started with a problem they had regarding a state grant which is apparently their principal means of support.

"They have a 43-year-old younger brother who is mentally retarded and in their care. They promised their dying mother they would take care of him. He is mentally about three or four years old—plays with a teddy bear, etc. I was able to resolve their problem and also sent them a rocking chair they said 'Buzzy' (the brother) wanted for Christmas.

"They are an amazing pair. Nancy and I have received gifts since that time of their leather work and they truly are masters of the ancient Spanish art of leather engraving. I've shown their work to some specialty shops in the hope the gals could add to their income. Their work is so unusual that belts such as yours go for about $150."

Ronald Reagan's genuine concern for his less fortunate constituents developed into a regular sideline occupation for us. He made me responsible for making sure people who turn to him as a last resort were not turned away with a form letter, but rather brought to his attention. Then, somehow, whether it was through the state or his personal friends, he tried to be of help.

A very dear story involved a spunky nine-year-old Palm Desert boy who was very angry because he believed that the governor had cut his mother's welfare check just before Christmas. "Don't you know," he said in his letter to the governor, "that I don't have a father and my mother is disabled?" The governor, knowing that he had increased grants to the truly needy by tightening welfare eligibility standards, asked for an investigation. It was quickly determined that the boy was right—due to a clerical error his mother's income was inadvertently reduced.

Rather than merely settling for correcting the situation, he kept the family in mind and at the appropriate occasion asked Frank Sinatra, who resided near the boy, if he wouldn't like to play Santa Claus to this obviously deserving family. Sure enough, the response was "have beard, will travel." And Frank Sinatra, disguised with dark glasses, paid a personal call on this family, making sure he knew exactly the boy's great dreams and hopes. From the letters we subsequently received from both the boy and the mother, it was obvious that Frank Sinatra's legendary generosity provided for them a Christmas they will never forget.

In responding to the boy's first letter the governor hinted just a bit at what he had in mind. He wrote:

"I am truly sorry, Paul, about all the hardships you and your mother have had to endure. With regard to the welfare cutbacks you mentioned, you probably were notified by now that the Department of Social Welfare has made a mistake. I trust that's all straightened out now.

"Your mother must be very proud of you, Paul. I have heard from several sources what a fine young man you are, and that is a continuing source of happiness to any parent. It also makes up, I am sure, for many of the things your mother has to go without now. I hope you will remain such a serious, good student—it is the best start to a bright and happy future.

"Don't lose your faith in Santa Claus. I have a hunch he won't forget you."

After Christmas, the governor replied thusly to a letter of thanks from the boy's mother: "I enjoyed hearing from you, and please tell Paul I appreciated getting his nice letter.

"Let me tell you there were Santa's helpers and they really are the ones who deserve the credit. The matter of correcting the mistake about your check was handled by the good people in my office. The Santa of the bike and other things was Mr. Sinatra, who was happy to have had a part.

"I've relayed your letter to all concerned, and they all say Happy New Year."

There was a time when the governor literally gave the clothes off of his back to a constituent who wrote to him,

"Will you please do me a little favor? I plan on getting married in about three months and I have been thinking maybe you would be kind enough to give me one of your used suits. I am very short of money now and I need a suit very badly. If you will do me this little favor I will thank you a million times."

Sure enough, the governor sent him a suit. And a letter came back: "Your beautiful suit came to me a few days ago and I wish to thank you a million times, it was a perfect fit and exactly my size."

In the letter the constituent disclosed his age. He was 80.

Once the governor received a letter from a soldier in Vietnam. It read: "In an attempt to find a dramatic way to show my wife how much I love her I would like to make what may be an unusual request of you—for you to deliver to her in person one dozen roses."

He hit the governor in a real soft spot. The governor wrote back that "I hope ... I can, in this small way, show you my personal appreciation for the sacrifices all of you are bringing overseas for the rest of us."

And one night Ronald Reagan delivered a dozen red roses to the soldier's wife with the words, "Hello. I'm Ronald Reagan. Your husband asked me to deliver these flowers to you and tell you that he loves you."

The governor's soft spot for GIs overseas came through again when, on a visit to Vietnam, a young man who flew him in a helicopter handed him a note asking, "Could you please tell my parents that I'm all right?"

On his return home Governor Reagan wrote: "Nancy called your mother on our first day home. They had a nice visit and, I'm sure, a good cry together. Your mother is looking forward to your Christmas homecoming. She also told of your work with regard to the drug problem. May I just say a thank-you on behalf of all of us for that as well as what you are all doing in our behalf."

The governor was one of those who wore a POW/MIA bracelet with the name of missing in action Marine Captain Stephen Hanson. In 1973, when it was discovered that the man had been killed in action, the governor wrote to his widow, Carole, "I know there are no words that can be helpful at a time like this. Nancy and I feel so deeply sorry, and yet we know, too, there is a mercy in knowing definitely as you now know.

"This noon Nancy dedicated a display case in the corridor of the capitol, which will be a memorial to all of the men who were prisoners and missing in action. She placed the bracelet I have been wearing in the case. I've worn it so long I feel as though I had a personal knowledge and friendship with Steve. For some strange reason I have a feeling without the bracelet on that I, too, shall miss him. I know Todd must be quite a big boy now. Much different than that little fellow that tugged at my coat such a long time ago. None of us know the why of God's plan for us, but surely part of Steve's sacrifice must be validated by the pride that Todd is going to be able to have in his father. I'm sure Steve would say now to you and Todd, 'The world is for the living,' and if his sacrifice is to mean anything you must find happiness to make it all worthwhile.

"Nancy and I send you our warmest regards, our sympathy, and affection."

Tragic occurrences also brought letters from the governor. In one case a man collapsed and died while waiting to greet his son who was arriving home from a North Vietnamese prison camp. He wrote to the widow: "I have learned of your tragic loss just at the moment of happiness when your son returned from captivity. I wish there were words that could ease your burden of grief, but of course there are none.

"Your mind must dwell on the fact that your husband was denied seeing his son return. Please don't think me presumptuous, but as a father he already had the joy of knowing his son was alive and well. If our belief in God assures us of anything, it is that he did indeed see his son's return.

"Some years ago in a little town in the Midwest, the father of the star player on the high school football team died the day before the season's big game. No one, of course, expected his son to play. The coach told him he shouldn't feel as if he had to play, but the boy told him he wanted to. That afternoon he played the best game of his entire career. When the game was over he told the coach this was the first game his father had ever been able to see him play. His father had been blind all his life.

"Whatever God's plan is for each of us, we can only trust in His wisdom and mercy. Forgive me for invading your privacy at this time and please accept my deepest sympathy."

The cancer death of a dear friend's son brought this letter:

"I do know that your faith will serve you now; your belief

124

that God does have a plan of infinite wisdom and mercy. It isn't given to us to understand at moments like this, we can only believe and trust in His goodness. Time will bring its healing, the pain will be less sharp, and you'll have memories that will grow warmer with the years. But those of us who care for you can only stand by, share some measure of your sorrow, and pray for that healing to come."

And the death of a slain policeman brought this letter:

"Words when you want and need them most seem very futile. Certainly I can find none to express my sympathy for you and my sense of personal loss and sorrow over the tragedy that has struck you and your family. I knew your husband in the kind of peculiar way that modern times have created between men of your husband's profession and those of us who are in public office.

"On a number of occasions he was one of those who provided security for me when I was in the area. It is true that such contact is only in passing with few opportunities for discussion or getting acquainted. Nevertheless, something else takes its place, at least as far as the protected is concerned. There is no way for me to describe the personal sense of gratitude and the real warmth I feel toward men like your husband who appear and are prepared to endure any risk to protect someone they have only just met. I am thankful we can still find such men in our land; without them, civilization itself would fail.

"I know your tragic loss must seem so senseless and without any rational explanation, but I have always believed that everything happens for a reason and that we must have faith in God's plan for all of us. It isn't given to us to understand—we can only have faith."

To a member of the Secret Service who lost a leg to cancer he wrote:

"I hope you won't mind my addressing you by your first name, but I've heard so much about you from Ed Hickey and some of the other fellows I know in the service that I just didn't feel I could be completely formal.

"They have told me of your operation, and I'm sure you must have some low moments when you wonder about the why of things. I don't know that I have any particular answers to questions of that kind, and yet from the vantage point of thirty-one years farther on, I have discovered that I believe very deeply in something I was raised to believe in by my mother. I now seem to have her faith that there is a divine plan, and that while we may not be able to see the reason for something at the time, things do happen for a reason and for the best. One day what has seemed to be an unbearable blow is revealed as having marked a turning point or a start leading to something worthwhile.

"From what Ed has told me, I know you need no words of encouragement about facing this. You have within you all the courage you need. Forgive me for sticking my nose in, but it's a privilege a fellow insists upon after he's gotten those other thirty-one years."

A Time for Planting

If the governor has one really soft spot in his heart, it's for children and young people. I can't recall the number of times all other business stopped or had to wait because he became involved with a group of youngsters having more questions than the governor had time on our calendar.

"Our biggest investment in the future is our kids," he gently explained to anyone who tried to hurry him when he was engaged in conversation with either one or a whole class of students, "and there is no time better spent."

A widely-hailed program instituted during his administration was a show called "Young People's TV." It was coordinated through the State Department of Education which selected at random groups of high-school students to meet with the governor in question and answer sessions twice a month. These shows were videotaped for later airing on campuses and on cable television.

It wasn't just the students who benefitted from this exchange of ideas. The governor freely admitted that these get-togethers were valuable to him. That he enjoyed them was obvious. Many times the end of the taping wasn't the end of the discussion, for he would invite the students into his office for more talk.

I used to marvel at the patience he showed on many such occasions. A few students came from conservative families and felt honored at the chance to meet their governor. Many came from low-income neighborhoods and couldn't wait to point aggressive, if not hostile, questions toward the governor. Some didn't try to conceal their prejudice and antagonism.

Nevertheless, the governor never reacted in kind. Instead he tried with a zeal rarely found in teachers to reshape and broaden their thinking. What often made it difficult for him was the students' basic ignorance about their government, the economy, and history. But his efforts were generally rewarded

127

as students who came with chips on their shoulders often left feeling the governor had dealt honestly and understandingly with them.

His disappointments—and there were some—came not when students continued to disagree with him but when once in a while they refused to acknowledge his sincerity or to give him credit for doing what he thought was right.

Perhaps I should not start out a chapter on a bad note, but there was one group of high-school girls whose churlish attitudes were reflected both in their first letters and in their replies to his letter. It was difficult for the governor to understand the rudeness and belligerence of these girls and he did not bother to respond to their second letters.

When the girls' first letters were called to the governor's attention he was appalled, not only at their ignorance, but also at the accusatory tone and antagonism in each. As a result, he wrote to the principal of the school saying that "I conclude that writing the letters to me was a class project. This is certainly the way responsible citizens should communicate their thoughts and questions to their elected leaders. . . . However, I am appalled at what else is being taught—or not taught—in this instance."

He pointed out that as the recipient of up to 10,000 letters a week he could not answer all of his mail personally, as the girls demanded. He added, however, that "I can and do choose those which merit personal attention. Normally I would say these do not, but I intend to answer each one of them if for no other reason than perhaps my letter will give them a better perspective than they have been given in the classroom. The spelling and grammatical errors in these letters, incidentally, are extremely interesting for a government class in high school. Especially so the misuse or misspelling of the word 'capitol'.

"The next time this teacher asks his or her students to write to a public official I believe he (she) would be well advised to stop and reflect: What will their letters reveal about what, and how, I have taught them?"

Each girl was sent a copy of that letter along with an individual response. The fact that the governor replied to them pleased them not at all. The fact that he wrote to their principal incensed them.

The girls' initial letters contained such sentences and phrases as:

"Just because you've got more money than a lot of people doesn't mean that you should completely ignore the subject (of the Homestead Act)."

"You won't get any votes out of me in the next election unless you get with it."

"I think you guys are just too lazy or are too busy with other things, like trying to raise income tax."

"I hate what you are doing. Either sitting in your office on some throne or in a private jet somewhere. We voted you in last time and now are voting you out."

"I have had it with the school system and it is worthless to me."

"By the time your [sic] up for election again I'll be abe [sic] to vote for you, but I wont [sic]!"

"With the way your [sic] going you wont [sic] get a damb [sic] vote out of me."

"The rate that things are going now, I hope you lose!!!"

"P.S. Start trying to improve or get out! Shape up! or ship up! [sic] I can really hurt you? [sic] Watch out in 74!"

One of the governor's replies will suffice.

"I don't know what grade you received in your high school class for writing your letter to me, but I'm afraid I have to give you a rather low grade on your understanding of government and which branch of government is in charge of things like the Homestead Act. The governor of a state can do nothing about changing the Homestead Act, since that is a matter of the federal government in Washington. If, however, you were referring to regulations limiting the value of property to be homesteaded under state law, I think you should know that you are completely wrong about the values you listed. The $12,500 limitation hasn't been in effect since 1963. In that year it was raised to $15,000, but last year (1971) I signed legislation increasing it to $20,000. You will note I said I *signed* legislation. This is not a matter that a governor can simply rule on; the legislature must introduce a bill and pass it by a majority vote in both houses. Then the governor has the right to either sign or veto.

"As for not getting any votes from you in the next election, I'm surprised that you haven't been told that when my term ends in 1974 I have stated publicly and repeatedly that I am not running for re-election.

"Now let's take up your point about pollution and how horrible the world is becoming. California's air-quality standards are the highest in the nation. In fact, we had to get special permission from Washington because our laws are more strict than the national laws. The same is also true of water pollution, and we have a program at work in California aimed at further cleaning our waters and certainly eliminating as much of air pollution as is possible. The truth is, while you perhaps don't recognize it on a smoggy day, we have made gains. The air is actually getting cleaner, but it will be of course a few years before it will become apparent. After all, we only discovered what causes smog a few years ago, and the scientist who made that discovery is employed by the state to try and find the answers to it.

"Now you speak of littering. Yes, it's true we have signs posted and we hope that citizens who see someone violating the law will take license numbers and report these citizens to us. It must be obvious to you that our highway patrolmen can't be every place at every moment when someone throws refuse out of a car window. But isn't this a problem that really finds the people at fault? Government doesn't litter the roadside or throw garbage in the river—people do—and the task is for people like yourself to spread the word until the vast majority of our people are as law-abiding in this as they are with regard to any other crime, such as stealing or murder.

"Then you say that I am either too lazy or too busy with other things like trying to raise income taxes. Again, you are hopelessly misinformed. I have just made a public announcement asking for a reduction of the income tax and promising if the legislature will not act, to allow the people to vote themselves a ten percent cut in the income tax. For four years I have tried to get tax reform that would reduce the homeowner's property tax. I have been balked by a small band of legislators who have refused to give the needed votes to pass this program.

"A great many people are saying things and writing things expressing views on public affairs. You will be better off if you realize there is usually more than one view on any such issue. Make sure you do not just accept one person's viewpoint. Find out for yourself what is the other side of an issue. The only way our system of government will work is with a well-informed citizenry—people who cannot be fooled by a column in a paper or a statement in a classroom, but will insist in finding out the truth of the matter for themselves."

130

The girls completely misread the governor's courteous gesture in sending them copies of his letter to the principal. Those who responded to him wrote in this vein:

"Now I would like to discuss why you sent these letters we wrote to *you*, were sent to Mr. Glaze with a letter, of which I received a copy. In *my* opinion you sent these letters back to our principal because you wanted to show us that our place in this world is sitting in our classes and keeping quiet. Well I am sorry, that is not how I intend to spend the rest of my life, sitting in some little corner and being quiet. If I think something is wrong I intend to let it be known, one way or another. If your intentions was [sic] to get any of us, including our teacher, into any trouble, then at least in my case there will be a fight. Maybe your intentions were to treat us like children by reporting us to our principal, instead I think you should be talking to us as young adults. Reporting us to our principal was a very childish thing to do."

The governor felt these second letters were best unanswered.

But these kinds of letters were rare. In contrast was a series of letters he exchanged over a period of two years with a high-school girl in his old home town of Dixon, Illinois. Her name was Petra Rusev. She was fourteen and a freshman when the correspondence began.

Petra began the correspondence with a cry for help. The Dixon high-school stage was condemned, the lights were bad, there would probably be no more plays, no more musicals on the stage where Ronald Reagan first began acting. Petra was determined to start a fund-raising drive to make it possible for the shows to go on.

"Please, Governor Ragan" [sic] she wrote, "would you help us out with a donation? I know this is a lot to ask of you but you see, you have a lot going for you and are famous. Can you help some of us get something going before all is lost?

"Nobody in the whole world knows that I wrote this letter because I want it that way. The only person's hopes that are high right now are mine. I love my school and want to do something for it. You probably did too when you went to DHS. I want to say too that if you help us there will be something nice to repay you for what you've done. Please! Please! Please! Try and help your old Alma Mater out.

"Please try and answer soon and also understand that I

131

will be overjoyed if you can help, but I will also understand if you can't. Think about it! Please! Thank you for your time.

"Bless you,

"Sincerely,

"Petra Rusev"

Petra was a new name to the governor. He wrote back to Mr. Petra Rusev:

"I remember everything about the plays I did in Dixon High and certainly know how you feel. I also understand those people who voted against a possible increase in their taxes. Sometimes hard decisions have to be made by grownups, and they are not always happy with what they have to do.

"Before I get back to your problem with the 'stage,' let me just point out some of the problems the people in Dixon, and in most of the rest of the country, have. Right now in California, taxes (federal, state, and local) take forty-three cents of every dollar the people can earn. The figure in Illinois is the same or very close to that. Now this means the average person works from New Year's until the first week in June just to pay taxes. Government is the biggest expense a citizen has. It costs more than food, clothing, and housing for a man's entire family. I point this out only so you won't have any bitterness about what the people of Dixon did.

"Now, about the stage and the plays you want to put on. Believe me, I agree that is a very wonderful part of your high-school experience. I'll restrain myself from any, 'what things were like' stories about D.H.S. in my day. I don't know what other facilities there may be in Dixon now that might be used temporarily. That is something you'd know better than I and something you might want to check on.

"Then there is another possibility—fund-raising—to get the money to repair the stage and make it safe. You've already thought of that as your letter indicates. This is really a possibility and you might be surprised at how many people would help once they knew the students were willing to work themselves to make it happen.

"Just yesterday, a glee club from a small college (250 students) in 'Pippa Passes,' Kentucky, sang here at the capitol in California. Pippa Passes is just down the road from Possum Trot—word of honor! The glee club is on a two-month tour of the country and they earned and raised $20,-000 to pay for the trip.

132

"I'm enclosing a check for $50. I wish it could be more. But, if you decide to try and raise the funds for the stage, use this as a first contribution and let me know how things work out."

Petra was thrilled as her return letter indicates. She signed it (Miss) Petra Rusev.

She also corrected her spelling of the governor's last name.

"Dear Governor Reagan," she wrote:

"How can I ever thank you for your kindness and thoughtfulness. You can also be sure that I understand about the taxes too. Important decisions have to be made, and I guess they're just not the way you want them sometimes.

"I had quite a time keeping the good news in me when I received your letter and check. I was just tickled to death! I did tell one person besides my family though and that is a girl who is very much interested in acting also. She and I are going to work together to get this show on the road.

"Today Jenny and I went to talk to Mr. Wiltz, our choral director. You should have seen his mouth drop open. I think he lost his words all together. After we discussed it with him, we went and talked to Mr. Boyer, our principal.

"Mr. Boyer's reaction was the same. We had a long talk and this is what we decided. Jenny and I are going to appear before the board and present everything to them. After their approval (which I'm sure we'll get), we are going to start all kinds of fund-raising and your check is the first donation and the base of everything.

"The Dixon station is going to keep a day open for people to call in and pledge money. We are also planning to collect money in town, door-to-door, and at the next choral concert. That is the plan Jenny and I have made and I can't wait for suggestions from the other students. I just have to keep my fingers crossed that all goes well at the board meeting.

"Thank you! Thank you! Thank you! That is all I can say because I am *so* grateful. You can be sure that I will keep you posted on what happens. You really are a great man!"

On February 16, 1973, the governor responded:

"I can't tell you how happy I was to receive your letter and to hear of your plans. You have a great opportunity now to prove what the people can do on their own without always having to go through government channels and fund things out of taxes.

"You'll probably have many discouragements. Anyone who is trying to enlist aid and support for a good cause does, but keep after it. At the end of the road, I'm sure there can be success and all that you have hoped for.

"I would appreciate it very much if from time to time you would give me a progress report and let me know how you're doing. You didn't mention the newspaper. I hope it will be included in your plans because it can be a great help in letting people know of your undertaking.

"Best regards."

Petra and Jenny did indeed appear before the Board of Education and their appearance resulted in a story in the *Dixon Telegraph* headed "Reagan's check launches fund drive to remodel DHS auditorium." The story noted "the check from Reagan was not a rubber-stamped document, but handwritten on the governor's personal account."

The clipping, sent by Quincy Adams of Dixon, brought this letter from the governor:

"Just a line to thank you for sending me the story from the *Telegraph*. I didn't know there had been any public reaction to my correspondence with Petra Rusev so I enjoyed seeing the paper. Incidentally, from her letters she must be quite a nice young lady, and the Dixon schools are doing a good job it would seem."

Petra wrote him again on March 4.

"Dear Governor Reagan,

"Thank you so very much for your last letter which you sent to me. I get so excited when I receive a letter from you. I have a lot of good news to tell you.

"We had our midwinter choral concert last week. Mr. Wiltz told the people that we were taking donations for the auditorium fund and we would greatly appreciate it if they would give. The people were more than happy to give. We had a girl stationed at each exit and when the people were all gone, every box was full.

"We collected a total of $241.23. This was pretty good because there really weren't too many people there. Three clubs also gave us a check for $25 which come to $75. This, along with your check and the 60 marks my grandmother sent from Germany, now gives us a total of $386.23, which we think is pretty good for only collecting one time.

"We are in the process of forming a committee to arrange collection dates in town, door-to-door, and then people may

134

also call in over WSDR, which is a radio station, and pledge money. Mr. Wiltz is pretty busy right now, because the tryouts for the musical are coming up. I'm going to see to it that the committee meets before tryouts because we want to get things going and not let them go to sleep.

"I'm sorry I forgot to tell you about the paper. It was truly a big help in publicizing the matter. I was pretty famous the day after the board meeting. I am enclosing the article that was in the paper about your check. I will also be happy to write you from time to time and tell you how things are going."

And again the governor replied:

"Dear Petra:

"This is the end of a long, busy day, so I'll just drop you a line to say how delighted I am to hear of your progress. I know you have a long way to go, but keep trying, get others involved, and above all don't get discouraged."

In mid-May there was a letter of discouragement from Petra. Nothing was going right. The adults were too busy with other things to show any interest. She was not allowed to seek donations at school events where admission was charged. "I'm so very mixed up that I just can't think straight anymore. I don't want to give up, but sometimes I feel as if it's the only logical thing to do. . . ."

In response, the governor wrote to his old friend, Ben T. Shaw, of the *Dixon Evening Telegraph*:

"Dear Ben:

"Maybe this should be a letter to the editor. Anyway, I have a problem, and I'm turning to you for help.

"Sometime ago I received a letter from a Dixon High School student, Petra Rusev, telling me of the need for repairs to the 'stage' the students use for their plays. She was upset with the failure of a bond issue to pass and reminded me of how important a play had been to me once on the Dixon High School stage.

"I didn't need that reminder because I still think that much of what has happened that is good in my life began in the old Northside High School when I first 'trod the boards' in Phillip Barry's play, *You and I*, under the direction of B. J. Frazier.

"In replying to her letter I suggested starting a fund-raising drive and told her she'd be surprised at how many people would help once they knew the students were willing to work themselves to make it happen. She took it from there and

135

with great enthusiasm set out on that course. I know your paper gave a boost because she sent me the clipping, also the most recent photo of her receiving a check from Mrs. McLennan of the American Legion Auxiliary. (Petra and I have kept up a correspondence!)

"My problem is her most recent letter. She hasn't faltered in her effort to get help for what seems like a most worthy project. Now, however, she seems pretty much alone in the crusade. The apathy which you and I know so well has set in after an enthusiastic start. Oh, she is still trying, the apathy is on the part of others, and to a young lady her age the goal seems discouragingly distant.

"Ben, she's trying to do what you and I have believed in so long. She hasn't joined that ever-growing crowd who look to government as the giver of all good things. Her letters have been heartening accounts of progress and cheerful acceptance of setbacks. But it's been a long stretch and the term is ending. Can you really afford to let her and those other young people fail? It's almost like saying, 'Don't try—just wait for a government handout of some kind.'

"I know from her letters that many of the good people of Dixon have helped, but what of the others? Is there a way to arouse their interest? That's my problem, Ben. I know it's a long way from Sacramento, but I've never felt all that far from the Rock River—especially when summer's coming on."

Mr. Shaw reported back the following:

"Your letter of May 31st about the remodeling of the Dixon High School stage has been discussed with Arnold Lund, our general manager, and Robert Nellis, city editor. Two reporters, Leonard Ingrassia and Tom Shaw, my grandson, interviewed Miss Petra Rusev about the stage needs and problems of getting money to have the work done.

"Miss Rusev wants new lights, new curtains, cushions for audience seats and rehabilitation of rooms under the stage. She tackled these problems at a time when the principal and school board were very busy with students in the final period of the school year. These administrators will have a meeting in about two weeks and then plan the fund drive. We will send copies of the papers with news stories so you will know the results.

"Ronald, you have delighted this young girl with your thoughtfulness in encouraging her to work for this program. I think she is of Russian descent, and then her folks came

136

from Germany. Her father is dead. Miss Petra Rusev is thrilled to know someone as busy as the governor of California would take the interest to send money from the request of a stranger. She shows your letters to everyone she talks with. I agree with her."

The governor sent a copy of his letter to Mr. Shaw to Petra. And in July she wrote:

"How can I ever thank you for your thoughtfulness! When I read your letter to Ben T. Shaw, it just made me cry. It made me realize how much you really care. I just wish all people were as considerate as you."

She went on to tell how the *Telegraph* was going to help with the project and how it had been decided "to kick off the new school year with the fund drive for the auditorium. We figured that this would be a chance where all the students would be back and wanting to do something together."

She concluded: "I want to thank you again for everything that you have done for me, to help me, and to help our auditorium. I just love you for it. You're really one of the greatest men that ever lived. Thanks to you I have hope again, and this time I know I'm not going to give up. Thank you! Thank you! Thank you!"

After school began Petra wrote again, describing her recruitment for the drama club, and the club's publicity and fund-raising efforts for the auditorium.

Before closing she wrote:

"I want to thank you so much for all the help you have given me. Several times I have felt like giving up, but your letters have always given me a lift, and the courage to go on. Thanks a million!!!"

The governor wrote back:

". . . you'll come to realize fund-raising is not easy. There are many worthwhile causes competing with each other for the money people have to contribute and it is drudgery and hard work, but you seem to be covering all bases. I don't know anything that I could suggest now beyond what you're doing, exploring every possibility. You might think in terms of cans with slitted tops through which people could insert money stating what they're for and seeing if merchants would permit them to be placed in their places of business so that people could drop a coin in on their way in or out. One other thing might be helpful; if either in the paper or in some public place in town, say at the main intersection, you could

137

mount a kind of thermometer that would show each week the level of funding with the figure of the amount actually needed. To watch the thermometer climb might serve as a reminder to people and they may get the idea of wanting to help see the thermometer reach the goal. . . ."

By November 4, the fund drive had been held and Petra wrote that "we now have a total of $3895.68 but," she noted, "the lighting board costs approximately $13,000 and I have no idea how much the area under the stage costs. The roof also leaks and the coat of paint that is now on the auditorium walls is the original.

"I really hope that we use the money and put it to use soon, because I feel that the people want to see something done with it.

"I am envied by a great many people," she continued. "I also hope that we can still keep up a correspondence such as we have been doing. It makes me so happy to be able to write to you. . . . We here in Dixon all love you!!!"

The governor responded:

"Congratulations! You've done a fine thing. I'm sure you've learned a great many things too. You've found out that good things just don't happen; there have to be people willing to make an extra effort to cause them to happen. I hope you've also learned that people are basically good and want to help.

"It's been a long road from that first letter when you were so disappointed about the bond issue to the happy letter I've just read.

"Now, why don't you sit down with the school authorities and see what is the top-priority problem in the auditorium that can be solved with the money you've raised? All of us all our lives have to do that—even governments. There is always more that needs doing than we can afford at any one time so we do it step by step. You've proven it can be done, others will be encouraged by your example to take up the cause in the years ahead."

By Thanksgiving Petra had written that an anonymous donor had given $1,000 to the drive. "When Mr. Boyer the principal told me, I was so happy I started crying. Then the Lions Club gave $250, the FHA gave $100, FFA gave $25 and things are really looking bright. It's all thanks to you, Governor Reagan." She signed it "One of your many fans" and P.S.'d, "I hope you had a very nice Thanksgiving. You couldn't deserve it more."

And so the letters continued. Petra reported the fund up to $8,000 and that the school board decided to buy a new lighting board without tapping the fund. The governor responded to one letter, "Since your letters of late have only been filled with good and exciting news, they have become regular day-brighteners. Thanks for sharing all the wonderful things that have happened."

In the following October came further news: "The auditorium is absolutely beautiful! We have added so very much to it. The sound system is getting finished up. We have the complete new ventilation system. We have gold wall-to-wall carpeting and brand new gold curtains. The whole auditorium has been repainted in a beautiful gold and white. The new lighting board isn't completely installed, but it's getting there. You wouldn't believe the change, Governor Reagan."

She concluded: "I'd like to end by saying thank you again for all the help you have given me, and the many words of encouragement when I was so close to giving up. I'll never be able to repay you. We've come so far and still have a long way to go, but now I know we can do it. I have to go now, cause it's getting late. Take care and God bless you.

"Love, Petra."

The governor's letter of reply was a little nostalgic. "By the time you receive this, a new governor will have been elected here. It's really hard to believe my term is at an end . . . your days sound busy and full of excitement. Take full advantage of these times. I know my school days bring back many good memories, and they seem to go much too fast."

That was the last of the letters while Ronald Reagan was governor. But the correspondence continues. I hope it goes on for as long as they both live.

Petra was unusual in that she became a regular correspondent with the governor. Most of the young people wrote only once or twice. Once in a while one would send along a little gift. Deborah Westrick of Fresno sent him "a doll I made of you. Inside is a story of your life. I think you're a very important man. I don't know what you look like but I tried my best to make you like you really are." The doll has black yarn for hair and eyebrows, and buttons for eyes. It has no ears. But inside is, indeed, a story of his life, beginning, "Ronald Reagan was a one-time motion picture star," and ending, "He is our present governor and has done a tremendous job."

A young man, whose parents were long-time friends of Ronald Reagan, wrote the governor that despite his affection and regard for him he felt the Republicans as a party lack compassion and therefore he had joined the Democratic party.

The governor, a Democrat himself most of his life, wrote a lengthy reply:

"I appreciate your letter and your motive in wanting to write me, but will not deny I am disappointed. You certainly have every right to choose your course, and my personal regard for you will be unaffected by your decision.

"We have a two-party system. It can only exist if people belong to each of those parties and the parties themselves stand for something. Now, however, at the risk of seeming to contradict myself, let me touch on the reasons you have given for your change.

"First, your commendable compassion for the black and the poor. I will take second to no one in my criticism of these past decades of so-called welfare. Not because of lack of compassion, but because those in charge were willing to create a class of people hopelessly mired forever in the swamp of permanent dole or handout. In our state, I am sure you are aware of the tremendous efforts we've made to break this pattern. What you can't know about is the frustration over these last two years of having a Washington bureaucracy throw obstacles in the way of our every effort to find a new method of helping. This, of course, touches on the racial issues as well.

"Do you know that the national average of black unemployment to white is 2½ to 1? Do you know, also, that in the great Los Angeles-Long Beach industrial area, we've reduced that ratio in these last two years to 1.4 to 1?

"Perhaps your feeling is due in part to the campus situation at San Francisco State where the issue has been successfully heralded as racial. There were approximately three hundred BSU [Black Student Union] members on strike. There have been and are about nine hundred black students going through the picket lines to attend classes. Many of them have taken beatings, threats to their lives, and vandalism to their cars and property. Whose side do I take?

"My administration has placed more Negroes and Americans of Mexican descent in executive and policy-making positions than any administration in the history of California. A number of these individuals have now been taken to Washington by the new administration. I'll grant you don't see many headline stories about this. Now, admittedly, I'm talking about California and my administration of more than two years. Shouldn't we keep in mind that Nixon has only been President two months? When I look back on my own first two months and realize how much more gigantic is his task of organizing an administration, I don't think it's possible to say at this point what direction he is taking, or what his policy will be. It's very difficult to speak critically of a victim of a tragic assassination, but I must point out that President Kennedy in two years hadn't succeeded in getting a single portion of his program through the Democratic Congress.

"You speak of the war and guns not being the answer, but do we know whether secret negotiations to end the war are going on or not? Obviously, if they are, we can't know about them or they are no longer secret and no longer effective. Certain journalists are on rumor expeditions, fishing for hints as to whether something of the kind is going on. Let me just add some history. It was a Democratic president who first ordered American combat units into the fighting, and it was his attorney general who said this was necessary to erase from the Russian minds any idea of our weakness as a result of the Bay of Pigs. I think someone could question whether that was enough of a motive for a war.

"But now, let me get to the real item of greatest concern to me, and based on our last conversation, of concern to you, also: Your generation and the communication gap. The schools grow bigger; government and the establishment grow bigger; and the young begin to feel they are numbers on a computer card.

"Who created this establishment? Whose philosophy over the period of your lifetime has consistently urged more and more government?

"For more than twenty years I've traveled the mashed potato circuit arguing for less government and more individual freedom. Over that same period, I have been attacked as a reactionary because the prevailing philosophy has been that only big government can have the answers in this complex world. How do I go about communicating with your generation? I've had campus editors, student body presidents and student groups here in the office. I correspond with students who have written to tell me they fear discrimination by teachers and administrators who favor those who would radicalize the campus. I'd like nothing better than to speak on the campus and have the kind of question and answer sessions we had during the campaign, but you know what would happen. The dissidents would make it impossible for me to communicate as they have with other speakers, cabinet members, and even the Vice President.

"The other night, I heard Humphrey on the Joey Bishop Show answering a question about campus disorders. I thought he described the dissidents as being two groups: a hard inner core of outright revolutionaries bent on destruction, surrounded by a larger group of misguided students who sincerely believe they are promoting a legitimate cause. There was more, but all of it was virtually word for word what I have been saying for quite some time. Yet, less than a year ago, this same Humphrey was holding me up to ridicule for saying exactly this.

"You say guns are not the answer on the campus. Of course not. But do you know of the hours I've spent in regents meetings and in conferences with university administrators begging them to take the firm action only they can take to solve these problems? When force must be sent to the campus, it is made necessary by their failure to use their own power, their own regulation to settle these issues. Then, faced with physical assault on other people, arson, bombing, destruction of property, the law must be called in. It is not true that the police escalated the action when the university finally asked me to declare a state of emergency at Berkeley. Wheeler Hall already had been burned down. Hundreds of thousands of dollars in damage had already been done. Students had been beaten by literally lynch mobs for simply trying to attend class.

"You speak of compassion—and, Steve, the announced causes of the campus disturbances are so often in the name of love for the downtrodden—but compassion is broader than just a theoretical concern about the disadvantaged. Twenty students caught a campus policeman alone and beat him and kicked him as he lay on the ground until he was hospitalized. Did they feel compassion? Did even one of them, for a second, look at his face there on the ground, wonder about him, wonder if perhaps a wife at home was preparing a meal for his homecoming? Wonder perhaps if he himself didn't have children, which incidentally he did, and whether they called him 'dad,' depended on him to help them with their homework and fix a broken toy?

"I have said over and over again that many of the announced causes of the campus disorder are worthwhile suggestions and could very easily be implemented. And I would favor implementing—but, Steve, the one issue that makes this impossible is when any group takes to the street and then with the threat of violence or coercion says 'Meet our demands, or we burn the place down, or prevent others from getting an education.' There can be no orderly society or respect for the rights of the individual if any administrative body or government body establishes the precedent of giving in to such a demand. This is like the first payment to a blackmailer. Once you embark on that path, what group, with what demand, might be outside next week?

"I listened for two hours while the university administration told me how terribly complex the campus problem was, how complicated it was to try and discipline those who were administering the beatings, breaking the windows, planting the bombs. Finally, I asked one question: 'How complex would it be if the mob outside was under the auspices of the Ku Klux Klan?' I have an uneasy feeling they would know how to handle this in about three and a half minutes. In short, I am charging that their own, so-called liberal philosophy, making them sympathetic to the announced aims of the riots, blinds them to their responsibility to offer protection to the others on the campus.

"Well, this has been a very long discourse, I know, and perhaps should take place in conversation, and not in writing. I suppose I am concerned, not about your right to choose a direction, but because your reasons for the change are not valid in the face of what seems to be the continuing big-government philosophy of the party you have chosen.

"Steve, in a few days I'll be meeting with the student body presidents of the campuses and yet, not one of them was elected by as much as ten percent of the student body. Is this a recommendation for lowering the voting age? Are we not justified in suggesting, first, that the student body in much larger numbers handle some of their own affairs, such as the election of student government which has in its hand the power to expend millions of dollars of compulsory dues? Could I suggest that perhaps the majority of the students start making their own views known about the violence and the disruptions on the campuses, instead of simply bypassing it as of no concern?

"And lastly, let me just say, I'll return to the Democratic party, too, if and when that party's philosophy recognizes once again the preeminence of the individual, the limitations on what government can accomplish, and the necessity for turning to the people themselves for help in solving the great social and human problems. . . .

"If I continue this letter another page and a half, it will have to be bound as a book, so I'd better quit here. One of these days, I hope we can have a talk."

Many young people wrote to ask him about his job as governor. To one he replied: "You ask how it feels to be governor and is the work hard? That is not as easy to answer as you might think. You know many hours of frustration as governor when things you think should be done are delayed or halted by petty politics, but you also know many days of great satisfaction and a sense of accomplishment." He ended: "This job is so challenging and so exciting that I haven't missed my other profession at all."

The letters from young people covered the broadest possible spectrum, as can be seen from the following excerpts:

A young man asked him what word he found most objectionable. His answer:

"As I thought more and more about your request I sat back and let my mind go as to just what word jolts me the most and, curiously enough, it turned out not to be one of those obscenities. I do not mind the use of profanity in a dramatic production or literature when it is appropriate, and I mean by this the usual words of 'hell' and 'damn,' etc. I find, however, that when God's name is invoked and tied to one of those words, it is very jarring. Profanity, as we all know, is a substitute for a lack of vocabulary, but the use of the name of God in connection with that is a violation of one of the commandments. I had not realized how strongly I felt about it until you asked your question.

"Strangely enough, in the old days of vaudeville, which was somewhat ribald, vaudeville comics would use the words 'damn,' 'hell' and others, but there was an unwritten rule of show business then; they never used the word 'God.' I wish we could return to that custom."

144

A young lady who was a Stanford University journalism student wrote him a complimentary letter. A pleased Governor Reagan wrote back that "you were very kind. . . . It might interest you to know that you are the first student of all the journalism classes I've met with who ever wrote such a letter. Please know that you brightened my day considerably."

He added, "If you'll forgive my rewarding you for your kindness with some unsolicited (and probably unnecessary) advice—search for the truth always; see if there is another side to every issue."

Another young lady asked him about the method of selecting presidents and vice presidents. ". . . we seem to have done pretty well with the system as it is," he responded, but continued: ". . . I have not, until now, given any serious thought to how the system could be changed. We might look at the position of the vice president, or candidates for that job, as men running for the presidency, going into primaries and soliciting the people's support. Having been chosen by the people in the primary, I would then suggest that the president and vice president run as a ticket as they do today to obviate the possibility of having a president of one party and a vice president of the other.

"If we were to go to a national primary as you suggest, and incidentally so many states are now having them we almost have a national today, we should be very careful to not change the voting system to where we have a president chosen by national popular vote. If this should come about, it might destroy once and for all our system of fifty sovereign states banded together into a federation.

". . . we should strengthen, rather than weaken our federated system. Few people realize what a great protection of freedom there is in the present system. The fact that anyone at any time can move across a state line is a protection against tyranny in state government. . . . For that reason, we should also be on guard against further centralization of authority in the nation's capital."

Many times answers to letters from young people found the governor stating and in a way renewing his own strong love for and faith in America and our system of government. He was not hesitant to point out errors we have made but the love always came through. This letter to Carrie S. Palmer is an example:

"Dear Carrie:

"Thank you for writing and for giving me a chance to express myself on the matters that concern you. You describe yourself as a 'common person' and again later refer to the 'common people' of America. Carrie, in one sense we are all common people in this country in that we have no inherited aristocracy. But, in a much more real sense we are a most uncommon people. Some of us go back in our family history to the very beginning of this nation and some of us are the first in our family's history to be Americans. In between is a mixture of those whose parents, grandparents or great-grandparents migrated here from every corner of the world. But, we all have one thing in common, we or our ancestors had a quality that set us apart from others in those countries of our origin. That quality was a love of freedom and the courage to pull up roots and cross an ocean to start over again in a strange land, where in most cases even the language was foreign. Together we have created a nation and a people known as Americans—a very special breed by any measure.

"Yes, we have some problems and they aren't helped by penny-ante politicians who seek to advance themselves by casting blame on others for those problems. Some in the press and on radio and television have found it is easier to get attention by throwing rocks than by talking of our accomplishments. Don't let them sell America down the river—there is much to love and be proud of in our country.

"Oh, we've made mistakes—many of them, and some of them explain in part the very problems that upset you. For several decades we've drifted into a habit of turning to government for solutions when we should have worked out the answers ourselves. Young people think government should provide a free college education. Big corporations ask government to protect them and wind up complaining when government begins to make management decisions they should have made themselves. Labor asks congress to regulate wages and institute social reforms that labor and management should be working out between each other. Farmers and dairymen ask for help and end up with a program of government regimentation—told what they can plant and what prices they can charge. And, yes, your father, like everyone else, finds government taking half of his pay check to pay for all the bureaucracy it takes to do things we should be doing for ourselves.

"The meat shortage resulted in part from government in-

146

terference that led to high feed and grain prices which in turn increased the cost of raising sheep, cattle, hogs, and poultry. Add to that, however, some acts of nature that can't be blamed on anyone. Two years ago, when the beef we are eating now were calves, there was a drought. These calves had to be fed hay and grain because the pasture had dried up. Thus, the farmers' cost in raising them doubled. Then last winter, we had severe storms in the West—one hundred million dollars worth of cattle were lost in one blizzard alone in Texas.

"On top of this (and this also explains the energy crisis) we are no longer the only people rich enough to eat meat, drive automobiles, and use oil and natural gas for heat and power. Japan, West Germany, and other nations are competing with us to buy things that are in short supply. Remember in the last fifteen years we increased our eating of beef from eighty-five pounds a year per person to one-hundred and sixteen pounds. Add to that the new markets in those other countries, and we just weren't producing enough beef. The same is true for oil and gas, as more people in the world could afford to drive cars.

"But, Carrie, we made it possible for those other people to live better—made it possible because Americans are the most generous people on earth.

"When World War I ended we cancelled much of the debt owed us by the European nations. We saved tens of millions from starving with outright gifts of every kind of supply. When World War II ended we literally rebuilt the industries and cities of not only our allies but of our enemies as well. Today the industrial power of West Germany and Japan bears a 'made in America' trademark. In the 1930s when Tokyo was leveled by an earthquake it was the United States that went in and helped keep them from starving. No matter where disaster has struck in the world—famine in China and India, floods in Europe and Asia, etc., our country has gone to the rescue without asking anything in return.

"Can you find one instance of anyone coming to our aid? We, too, have had destructive floods on the Mississippi and the Ohio, tidal waves in the gulf, hurricanes and earthquakes. Never have we asked for help and none has been given.

"We speak of five major wars we've been in, but actually we've committed military forces to action 158 times in our

147

197-year history. Most of the time, we did so to help someone else—someone weaker whose freedom was threatened.

"Carrie, today young people are being taught a great many things that aren't true, and I'm afraid you are going to have to dig out the truth for yourself. Mistakes we've made—most of them well intentioned ones—but we'll correct them, from the meat shortage to being in a position where we can be blackmailed by the Arab oil producers.

"Let's stop asking government to do things for us we should be doing for ourselves. Let's ask government to let us keep more of our own pay checks. And let us tell government and all those doom criers in our midst who want government to be a big brother to us all, that all we ask of freedom is freedom itself. This is still the one place on earth where a man can be whatever God intended he should be; where you can fly as high and as far as your own ability and effort will take you.

"You are absolutely right about this country and its dependence on men like your father. We read about knights in armor, or heroes doing battle, but the greatest unsung heroes in the world are men and women who get up in the morning, get you off to school, go to work, pay the bills, and voluntarily contribute to good causes in spite of high prices and higher taxes. They make this system work in spite of the demagogues and reformers who occasionally mess things up.

"And, Carrie, I have a hunch you'll be helping to keep that system working in a few more years. Your father should be a very proud man."

The same warm optimism came through in a letter to William R. Hammond of Schenectady, New York.

"Dear Bill:

"If I were 21, I believe, today, I would take a second and very good look at the world around me.

"If I had gained an impression in some classrooms, or from the daily fare doled out to us as news on too many TV newscasts, that we lived in a somewhat corrupt nation, that people were selfish and that all the old traditional values were long since outmoded, I would try to see if there wasn't another side to the coin. Optimism makes for a far better life than pessimism and there is much to be optimistic about in this land of ours.

"No matter how seamy the news may seem at times, this is a country of warm, generous people who seldom miss an opportunity to do good for their fellow man. In fact, the kindness of our people may have contributed to some of our troubles. We've tended to spoil our children and coddle our wrongdoers. But that's better than if the fault were the other way.

"I'd accept the help of those who wanted to help me and repay them by doing the same for others. I'd look with optimism and anticipation at a very exciting world that could be mine in the years ahead."

The environment and the ecology also drew letters from the younger generation. To Steven Hansch, editorial editor of *The Town Crier* in Santa Monica, he talked about "three kinds of pollution: actual, hysterical, and political:

"Hysterical pollution leads to political pollution with the result that all too often little or nothing gets done about actual pollution.

"Young people today can become a great force for good in overcoming the mistakes of the past and insuring that their children will live in a cleaner world. The great need is for calm appraisal, recognition and evaluation of the real problem, and practical realism in solving it.

"Let me give you some examples of hysterical pollution. A letter arrives on my desk signed by an entire schoolroom of eight-year-olds. They beg me to save them from smothering to death before they can grow up. Obviously they had been frightened into mailing such a letter by some adult who should know better.

"Another letter, again from school children, expresses a belief that very soon all the redwood trees will have been cut down and replaced by plastic imitations.

"Now let's look at the facts about both of these examples.

"First, air pollution. Yes, we have problems in some areas, particularly our cities, but they are better than they were in the past. Martha Washington, when she was the first lady of our land, wrote a letter to her daughter about the terrible air pollution in Philadelphia. She said a majority of the city dwellers had eye infections from the smoke and gases in the air. Even Cicero in Ancient Rome wrote of the joy in getting out in the country away from the poisonous atmosphere of the city.

"Our problem today is caused largely by automobile exhaust. But not too long ago every home had a chimney belching coal smoke every hour of every winter day. We only discovered that autos were the cause of smog a few years ago, and now we are doing something about it. Today's autos are only about a third as polluting as the cars of just eight or nine years ago, and our regulations require the manufacturers to virtually eliminate all pollutants by 1975.

"In the meantime we have political pollution. A politician wanting to attract attention introduces a bill to ban all autos if they aren't 100 percent clean within an impossibly short time. He knows that his proposed bill would force every car and truck off the road, close down the manufacturers, put every oil station out of business, and so on and on. Others have to rescue us from his demagoguery either by voting his bill down or by veto. He has made his splash, however, but in so doing has diverted the energies of those who are seriously trying to reduce air pollution.

"The same thing happens with regard to the trees. California over the years has done one of the outstanding jobs of preserving the great cathedral-like groves of redwoods. Almost 150,000 acres are now in our parks. Our lumber industry cutting the less spectacular commercial redwoods is rapidly approaching what is called 'sustained yield.' This means cutting no faster than the trees can grow back. But once again our energies are diverted from the real task of improving timber practices while we do battle with all sorts of unrealistic proposals. The plain truth is that we can have a lumber industry providing wood for home construction and furniture, and beautiful forests, too."

Molly C. Devine of Sacramento received this letter:

"I know you and your friends are impatient and want to get at the problem of pollution right away so my first answer won't make you too happy. Right now the main thing for all of you to do is study and learn about our environment but also about what we as people must have to make our lives enjoyable and fulfilling. This means jobs in which we earn our living, places to live, and power to heat our homes and light the lights.

"When you study, be sure to see all sides of each question and don't be frightened by those on either side of an argument who would have you believe the world will cave in if we don't do things their way. There isn't any problem we can't solve if we use common sense.

"Right now California is leading the nation in our efforts to solve the problems of pollution and environmental protec-

150

FOR A FREE BOOK, TURN TO THE BACK PAGES

tion. This doesn't mean we can let up or that the problems will be solved overnight. We'll need your help in the years ahead when you are ready to take your place as citizens.

"But now in the meantime, why don't you look around you—I mean you and your friends, of course. See if you can find projects in your neighborhood or even farther afield. Several days ago the TV news showed a school class that picked a small creek here in Sacramento and spent the weekend clearing it of junk and tin cans to make it once again a sparkling, clear stream. There are sections of roadway and river banks littered with bottles and cans. Perhaps you can find someone who will lend a truck for hauling the debris away. Is there an empty lot that has become an eyesore— would the owner let you clean it up?

"I appreciate your wanting to help and know you can. I'd like to hear from you if you find a project."

In response to a letter from Tanya Tatum asking how he stood the pressures of office, he wrote:

"When I was first seeking this office, I made a campaign promise that I would make every decision based on the idea that I would never again run for public office. Now this didn't mean I wouldn't, but rather that in making decisions I would weigh them on what I honestly believed was right or wrong and not on how it might affect votes in some future election. I have kept that promise.

"The other thing, Tanya, when I first got here and sat at the desk where I'm sitting now, I found when almost every hour someone stood across the desk from me and said we have a problem, I had an almost irresistible desire to look over my shoulder at times as if there might be someone there I could pass the problem on to. I found out I was looking in the wrong direction. Obviously, the final decisions had to be made by me, but, Tanya, the help I have found is in turning to God and asking His help in prayer. I believe very much in the power of prayer and feel if you sincerely ask for His help, it is forthcoming. For me that has been the answer."

Not all of the governor's letters about youth were to them. Some went to parents. One parent wrote to him that "we have created a generation in which an alarming majority choose to wear the mask of indifference or intolerance. . . .

"It seems obvious that a frightening percentage of youth is running away from life.

"While talking to a youngster who was on dope, I asked

151

what his parents thought of the way he chose to live. Consider, carefully, his reply: 'They don't give a damn what I do.' When asked why he thought that, he continued with, 'Not once has my old man or old lady said they would break my neck if they caught me smoking pot. They have never said they think my friends are creeps even though those thoughts are written all over their faces. I have NEVER heard my old man say, "Son, this is what I expect you to be like—this is how I expect you to act . . ." If they really cared, if they really loved me, they would help me. They don't give a damn and neither do I.' "

The governor's reply read:

"Let me get on the bandwagon with a counterpoint to the young pot smoker's plea or plaint. In New York recently at a dinner party a prominent editor sought the advice of several of us on 'What do you tell a teen-ager who uses pot?' I suspect he was really asking 'what do I do about my son?' I volunteered a few logical approaches, all of which he rejected. Finally (a little short of temper) I said, 'Why don't you tell him if you catch him with one of those things in his mouth you'll kick his bottom side up between his shoulders?' Of course, he rejected that too.

"Sandy, I'm convinced a lot of the college rioters are saying what your friend said. They really want someone to give them a set of rules and say 'don't step over that line.' "

A Sacramento school teacher wrote to him:

"I thought you might enjoy a little humor today which happened in my kindergarten class.

"I was briefing my class on the field trip we were to take the following day. One of the places scheduled to visit was the governor's mansion.

" 'Does anyone know who is the governor of California?' I asked.

"(Complete silence)

" 'Oh, come now children, you know his name. Ronald——?' (I hinted)

"Instantly twenty-three hands shot up and twenty-three voices shouted triumphantly—

" 'RONALD MCDONALD!' "

The governor thanked her, saying "I did get a kick out of it. I guess television just has more power than any of us know.

"I'll return the favor by telling you of the teacher who

taught her class about magnets and their properties and then several weeks later gave a test and asked them what it was that was spelled with six letters, began with an M and picked up things. Eighty-seven percent of the class said 'mother.' The true television anecdote, however, is the child who told her mother she liked her better than the other leading brands.

"Thanks, again, and please give my greetings to your class. Tell them I don't mind being Ronald McDonald at all."

The governor also presumed upon his friendship with the President on behalf of young constituents.

"Dear Mr. President:

"I am enclosing a letter regarding a special tour you provided for some of our mutual constituents. The son, Bob, he refers to had his eighteenth birthday. He is a paraplegic, paralyzed from the chest down in an accident about four years ago, a high school senior. The Gibsons are strong, loyal Republicans.

"Now, having said thanks, I reward you with another chore if you see fit to do it. A little nine-year-old girl, Carol Ann Poitevin, Painted Valley Stables, 2940 Chestnut Avenue, Long Beach, California, 90806, has a mare stabled at the horse farm next door to the Western White House. It is due to foal momentarily. Carol feels this makes her a next-door neighbor to you. She is sure you must have reached over the fence and petted her mare sometime when you were out there. She would like a note from her neighbor that she could keep."

Here is one other letter to a parent who was also a friend.

"Dear Bing:

"Last Friday, as you've no doubt seen in the news, I had a rather busy time at the University of California at Santa Cruz. There is no need for me to go into the sad experience of seeing students on that beautiful campus rioting, threatening physical harm to the regents assembled there, and cursing the regents with profanity and unrepeatable obscenities. Enough to say—it happened.

"But out of all this came one bright moment, at least for me. On the bus tour of the campus, students have been assigned to the buses as guides. I found myself seated beside one of the nicest, most ladylike young women one could hope to meet—your daughter. After hearing her good common-sense reaction to all that was going on, I finally had to ask how she had been able to maintain such a sense of values in the atmosphere so prevalent there. She stated very simply, 'That's the way my mother and father raised me.'

"You must be very proud and you have every right to be."

An eleven-year-old girl who wanted a horse desperately wrote to the governor explaining that her father could not afford to keep it at the stables "and I cannot keep it in my yard in Long Beach." At her father's suggestion she asked "if I could graze my horse on your pasture in Malibu. My dad said it might be tax deductible. I am eleven years old and my dad said you would understand. Please Mr. Reagan write back soon so I will know the answer."

The governor wrote back:

"I certainly can understand how you feel; horses have been a large part of my life and I love them as you do. But your father has brought up a very important point. They can't be stored away in a garage like a bike until you feel like going for a ride, and there is an ongoing expense day in and day out. Unfortunately we have had to sell our ranch so I can't be of help in the way you suggested.

"But let me make some other suggestions. First of all, not owning a horse needn't keep you from riding and learning about horses. As a matter of fact, in the cavalry (which is where I learned to ride) you weren't assigned a horse of your own until you had learned to ride on many different horses—a different one every day.

"You have many years ahead of you to enjoy riding and to have your own horse. Indeed you'll know too the sorrow of saying goodbye because we do outlive our horses. Now and for the next few years, why don't you go to a stable (you probably ride at one now), ride many horses, learn to know their differences, and learn all you can about their care? Then when you are a few years older you might discover you can have a horse of your own, and you'll know better the exact kind of horse you want.

"At that time you can very probably make an arrangement with someone or some stable so that you can board or pasture your horse in return for helping with theirs. You'll know enough about the care of horses that you'll have something to offer.

"Being a father myself, I know how very much your father would like to be able to help you realize your dream, but sometimes we have to wait for the good things. If it will help to know this, I didn't have a horse of my own until after I

154

was grown up. You'll do better than that, so keep on riding and studying."

A young man suggested that a way to create rapport with the younger generation would be for the governor to start riding a motorcycle. The governor declined. "I ... think I'll have to stick to horseback riding. You see, there is the matter of security. When I go any place, I'm one of a group. We might look like Hell's Angels with all of us out there on motorcycles."

A campaign held by a high-school girl to save four acres of land for an ecological park brought this note from Governor Reagan. "I wish more people who are talking about saving the environment had your great good common sense." Enclosed was a check for $50.

Sometimes letters were never sent. A young California constituent wrote asking for a picture and a phone call. The governor dictated the letter, then did not sign it. Instead across the bottom he wrote to me: "Just send the picture. I'll call him—I'm a sucker."

And that is true—but only if having a soft heart makes a person "a sucker."

Laurie Rothe and Jeffrey Trauberman, the editors of *Embers*, a publication of Wayne Valley Senior High in Wayne, New Jersey, wrote to Governor Reagan asking him to write an article advising the school's graduating seniors. "You've taken quite a chance," he warned them, "risking a detailed and nostalgic accounting of things as they used to be, or a denunciation of things as they are."

But then he sent the following letter to the graduating seniors:

"Your editors have asked me to attempt some advice, particularly for those of you who are now leaving high school. Since all of us enjoy giving advice, I accepted their invitation with delight; also, I might add, with a feeling of appreciation for what I consider a very great honor.

"Now, after many false starts, and a waste basket full of wadded up rejects, I have discovered this is more of a challenge than an opportunity. Advising an individual with whom you are acquainted is one thing; generalizing across the generation gap is quite another.

"All of the clichés about entering a new phase in your lives have been strengthened by the change in voting laws. You are about to come into your inheritance of citizenship as full participants in the social structure—call it establishment if you will—virtually coincident with receiving your diplomas. I'm not sure that you greet this prospect with joyous anticipation.

"A consortium of doom-cryers made up of journalists, commentators, writers, and yes, a goodly portion of the educational and intellectual community, have conspired together to paint a picture of a sick society in a polluted land where money-grubbing materialism has replaced spiritual values. Admittedly, the world you inherit is less than perfect. Not all the problems of human misery have been solved. Poverty and inequality of opportunity still exist; prejudice and bigotry have not been erased from every heart; and war, man's greatest stupidity, still takes place.

"But let my first advice to you be, look beyond the picket signs and leaflets; check the doom-cryers' pronouncements against the facts. Each generation stands on the shoulders of the one that has gone before, and as a result, each succeeding generation can see farther and more clearly because of the height from which they gaze. If you will look from unprejudiced eyes, you will discover ours is not a sick society, and there is much to be proud of in this land and much to love.

"Man has known only a few moments of freedom in his entire history, and most of those moments have been ours. Half the economic activity in all history has taken place in America, and we have shared our wealth more widely than any people who ever lived. Ninety percent of the people in our land lived in poverty at the time of my birth; today it is ten percent. More than two-thirds of our people lived in substandard housing; today, it is less than ten percent. Our poor have miracles of convenience not even a king could afford a hundred years ago. Ninety-nine percent of our homes have refrigerators and gas or electric stoves; ninety-five percent have television; more than ninety percent have telephones. In my lifetime we have eliminated diseases which had plagued man for thousands of years. I've already lived ten years longer than my life expectancy when I was born.

"Yes, we have ethnic and racial problems, but we've made progress. We have done more in a single lifetime to advance the dignity of man than had been done in all the long climb from the swamp to the stars. When my generation left high school we took our place in a society that didn't even know it had a racial problem. I'm proud that we were the ones who

156

said, 'This isn't good enough.' There is still a lot to be done, but also we've done a lot. In America today a higher percentage of our minority young men and women go to college than the percentage of white youth in any other country in the world.

"We are in an ugly war, but not because we don't love peace, and certainly not because we have an aggressive, hostile nature. My generation has known war four times and has learned to hate it. We long for peace, but know that longing is not enough. In this disturbed world it is possible to love peace, to strive for peace, and find yourselves in war. If this is hard for you to accept, ask yourselves what kind of a world you'd be living in if another generation had not been willing to bleed its finest young men into the sands of Omaha Beach, the mud of Normandy, and a thousand coral atolls up and down the Pacific. The inescapable truth is that the lasting values, the things which go to make up what we call civilization, have always been those things for which men have been willing to die if need be.

"With your idealism, your youth and energy, you are going to make this a better world. In your lifetime you will most likely see cancer eliminated, poverty further reduced, and those last pockets of bigotry and prejudice wiped out. You may in your lifetime realize man's dream of a world without war. Please keep striving for that, but not under the delusion that peace is worth any price.

"Challenge the mores and customs of the past, but do not discard them simply because they are of the past. A cynical few would have you turn away from old truths and moral standards accumulated by man through the ages. Select carefully the things you would discard. No nation which has outgrown its God has ever lived to write additional pages of history. This nation is in need of a spiritual reawakening, and a reaffirmation of trust in God. This can begin with a return to simple morality—a revival of honor and integrity in our everyday lives.

"If I read your generation correctly, you've been turned off by hypocrisy and dirty politics; you yearn for leaders who will be above partisanship and personal gain. Well, your leaders are among you now—presidents, governors, senators and congressmen, supreme court justices—how will you know which ones they are when the time comes to choose? Do you think they can cheat now, shave the rules, choose the laws

157

they'll obey or disregard, and then by some magic become men and women who will make decisions on the basis of what is morally right or wrong?

"One generation can change the course of history; can once again insure that this nation will be a shining golden hope for all mankind. An older generation hopes with all its heart you'll do this."

Love Letters, More or Less

While this is supposed to be a book of letters by and from Ronald Reagan there is a group of letters *to* him that I think must be included. These are letters from children, mostly written in his early years as governor. They are all written very seriously, but some make me want to laugh, and others make my eyes misty.

For a long time the governor wanted to find a way to share them with other Americans. Perhaps through this little book people, who otherwise would never have the opportunity to see them, will have a chance to share the pleasure that was the governor's when he received them.

"Dear Governor:

"I remember when you were an actor. Now I see you have changed.

"I liked you better as an actor.

"Your ex-fan,

"John"

"Dear Mr. Reagan:

"My daddy says that since you became governor, many things have changed.

"Two ice cream men used to come down our street every day—but not any more. One of the trucks was pulled by a horse. Did you take him to a race track or just change the streets they go down?

"Cindy"

"Dear Governor Reagan:

"Could you come and have a barbecue with us at our house. Our pool is 75 feet by 40 feet.

"You may, also, bring your family but my Mom says you can't spend the night."

"Dear Governor Reagan:

"Yesterday I saw a bumper sticker that said "Ronald Reagan eats peanut butter.

"I want to know if it's true.

"Kathy Johnson

"P.S. No offense"

"Dear Sir:

"February is Citizenship Month.

"What ideals, habits, and attitudes did you develop as a third grader which helped make you the outstanding citizen you are today?

"Thank you.

"Love,

"Becky"

"Thank you very much for just the information I needed. But there is one thing I don't understand. Specifically, what are you doing about it? Thanks again.

"I am very grateful for your answering my request. The signature on the letter you sent back, your own, I will keep it until I die, and I really mean it.

"From Margie"

"Dear Governor:

"How come when politicians have meetings about pollution and conservation, they are always in smoke-filled rooms?"

"Dear Sir:

"It is wonderful to know you are governor of California. This proves that any citizen can run and be elected."

"Dear Mr. Reagan:

"You are doing a terrific and outstanding job—and I am proud you were elected governor of Ohio.

"Your friend,

"Jackie"

"To my Governor:

"My name is Andy Peterson. I'm in the 8th grade and 13 years old. On my way to school I walk on 28th Street. When I get to the corner to go across, I can't see if any cars are coming because the trees are so big and lots of cars are parked on the side. This is very dangerous and before I get killed, I think something should be done about it.

"Thank you.

"Leslie Jamison" [sic]

"Dear Governor Reagan:

"I'm sorry you were killed last night on TV.

"My brother said you were faking. Is that true?

"Love,

"Lisa"

"Dear Governor:

"Some of us would like to know if a teacher can hit a child on the hands with a ruler.

"I say the teacher doesn't have the right to.

"Maria

"P.S. If my writing is bad—it's because my hand is sore."

"Dear Governor:

"I am a new citizen. My whole family is, too. We come from Mexico.

"More than anything I want a great American flag. I will love and care for it.

"Your new friend who loves you,

"Maria

"P.S. I will also treat it with respect."

"Dear Honorable Sir:

"I want to know if you think diagramming sentences is important later on in life. In fact our whole class wants to know if you had to diagram sentences in the seventh grade.

"Did it help you to speak?

"Sincerely,

"Wally

"P.S. I hate diagramming sentences."

"Dear Sir:

"I am in the 4th grade. This is a test on how to write letters. I think it's nobody's business how people write letters.

"Will you kindly do something about this?

"I am—

"Paul Turner"

"Dear Mr. Governor:

"Have you ever heard of the Dumbarton Bridge? If you have, could you maybe change the name, please? It would sure help me with the kids at school.

"Yours truly,

"Betsy Barton

"P.S. If you can't change the name—could you just take off the *Dum*?"

"Dear Mr. Reagan:

"I would like a picture of you and your family. I see you and your family on TV and in the newspapers and magazines. I know all about you. I am a big fan of yours. Thanks.

"Yours truly,

"Pam

"P.S. On the back name the people in the picture."

"Dear Governor Reagan:

"I need information right now on your running for president.

"Are you going to do it? What are your chances? Will you run?

"Thank you.

"Danny

"P.S. If you don't know can you give me an address where I could find out?"

"Dear Governor:

"What are you going to do to help California's Indians?

"Love

"Billy

"P.S. My father is an Orthodontist."

"Mr. Reagan:

"Before I get started—I warn you, I'm only a girl of ten—and a Democrat, too!

"Yours

"Lori"

"Dear Governor Reagan:

"I wrote you once before about having to go to school on my birthday—and nothing happened.

"My next birthday is a month away and I am wondering what your plans are.

"Let me hear from you soon.

"Jeff"

"To Mr. Ronald Reagan

"I pray for you every day because Mom thinks you need it.

"From Margie King"

A Free Book

1. **HOW TO START YOUR OWN SCHOOL**, Robert Love. Everything a parent or principal needs to know, by someone who did it himself. "An important and readable book that tells you how to do it"—*Human Events.* **$1.95**

2. **THE REGULATED CONSUMER**, Mary B. Peterson. *The Wall Street Journal* contributor shows how seven Federal regulatory agencies have been captured by the businesses they were supposed to regulate! How this hurts consumers everywhere, and what can be done about it. "This thoughtful, challenging book can perform a great service" —*Fortune.* **$2.95**

3. **THE DEFENSELESS SOCIETY**, Frank Carrington and William Lambie. A scathing look at how the Courts and Congress have tilted the battle against crime in favor of the criminal and against society, with proposals for restoring the balance. Frank Carrington is the author of *The Victims,* executive director of Americans for Effective Law Enforcement. **$1.95**

4. **THE CASE AGAINST THE RECKLESS CONGRESS**, Hon. Marjorie Holt, ed. Nineteen Republican congressmen contribute chapters on the major issues before Congress. All 435 Representatives' votes are recorded. "Not merely a naysayers political bible. The authors do offer alternative programs. Moreover, the book provides us with a chance to examine 'the conservative side' whether or not one agrees with it."—*CBS Radio.* **$1.95**

5. **THE MAKING OF THE NEW MAJORITY PARTY**, William Rusher. "If anyone can invigorate the ideological comradeship of economic and social conservatives, it is William Rusher. This is a well-written and thoughtful book." —*The Wall Street Journal.* **$1.95**

6. **THE SUM OF GOOD GOVERNMENT.** Hon. Philip M. Crane. "An arsenal of timely arguments against collectivist practice, demonstrating the superior virtues of the private market system in a dozen different categories. Mandatory reading."—*National Review.* **$1.95**

7. **THE GUN OWNER'S POLITICAL ACTION MANUAL**, Alan Gottlieb. "A practical guide to political participation. Offers indispensable advice to the novice contender in the opinion-making ring."—*Field & Stream.* **$1.95**

8. **SINCERELY, RONALD REAGAN**, Helene von Damm. The personal correspondence of Ronald Reagan as Governor

A Free Book

with every four books you order!

of California. Covers his views on almost every national issue. "There is much in these letters that sheds new light on the man."—*Saturday Evening Post.* **$1.95**

9. THE HUNDRED MILLION DOLLAR PAYOFF: HOW BIG LABOR BUYS ITS DEMOCRATS, Douglas Caddy. "An extensively documented exposé of big labor's illegal largesse."—*Newsweek.* **$2.95**

10. A NEW DAWN FOR AMERICA: THE LIBERTARIAN CHALLENGE, Roger MacBride. ". . . an intelligent, serious and persuasive advocate. We might all like to live in his vision of America."—*Philip Nobile.* **.95**

11. THE MUNICIPAL DOOMSDAY MACHINE, Ralph de Toledano. "Forced unionization of public employees threatens American democracy. Toledano's book is must reading" —*Ronald Reagan.* **$1.95**

12. JIMMY CARTER'S BETRAYAL OF THE SOUTH, Jeffrey St. John. "The examination of Carter's labor alliances, Carter's belief in central planning, and his philosophy of social reform are valuable."—*Dallas Times-Herald.* **$1.75**

13. WHY GOVERNMENT GROWS, Allan H. Meltzer. "A persuasive explanation of government bloat." (*Booklet*) —*Fortune.* **.95**

14. ADAM SMITH'S RELEVANCE FOR 1976. Milton Friedman. "Demonstrates the prescience of Smith."—*Evans, Los Angeles Times Syndicate.* **.95**